CHRISTMAS IN GEORGIA

CELESTINE SIBLEY

PEACHTREE PUBLISHERS, LTD.
ATLANTA, GEORGIA

Published by
PEACHTREE PUBLISHERS, LTD.
494 *Armour Circle, NE*
Atlanta, GA 30324

Manufactured in the United States of America

Design and illustration by Paulette Lambert

Library of Congress Catalog Card Number: 85-61978

ISBN 0-931948-83-5

BOOKS BY CELESTINE SIBLEY

The Malignant Heart

Peachtree Street, U.S.A.

Christmas In Georgia

Dear Store

A Place Called Sweet Apple

Especially At Christmas

Mothers Are Always Special

Sweet Apple Gardening Book

Day By Day With Celestine Sibley

Small Blessings

Jincey

Children, My Children

Young'uns

For All Seasons

CONTENTS

MIZ TIPPEN'S CHRISTMAS GUEST

(NOTE: This is a story which may or may not have happened in the year 1780 in what was then Wilkes County, Georgia. History will attest that Sukey Hart and her parents, Benjamin and Nancy Hart, lived and some of the events happened. As for the others, well, history doesn't say they *didn't* happen, does it?)

Chapter I

OLD MIZ TIPPEN WAS
waiting outside her cabin on Wewatchee
Creek that frosty morning in December 1780
when Sukey Hart came bringing her the last
of Ma's apples.

The old lady was blind but her ears were
sharp and the minute she heard Sukey's feet

hit the footlog she started flailing the air with her walking stick and calling out something in her high-pitched, cracked old voice.

"Hold your hosses, Miz Tippen," cried Sukey irritably. "I cain't hear a word you a-saying!"

The old lady subsided and Sukey concentrated on balancing herself on the log over the little creek without using her hands, which were both engaged in holding the apples in her apron. They were the best apples from the Hart orchard and it made Sukey a little mad that she had to tote them over to Miz Tippen's. But that was Ma for you, giving away the last thing she had.

"Ain't no use to save back nothing, Sukey," Ma had said. "What the thieving Indians don't get them murdering Tories will. I'm bound to choose who eats my apples."

And Ma had taken a basketful to the Continental soldiers who were encamped down on the river, waiting for a chance to take Augusta and Savannah back from the British. She had directed Sukey to take the rest to their blind neighbor, Miz Tippen. Mrs. Tippen's only son had been killed fighting the British for the American independence and now the Harts farmed her patch along with her own, sharing whatever they had. Mostly Sukey didn't mind. But the apples . . . they represented the only change in fare from taters and corn pone and wild game until the spring gardens would come in.

Still, her dark blue eyes softened as she lifted them from the footlog and rested them on Mrs. Tippen. She was a funny looking old thing in her bunchy black clothes, hopping about on the doorstep like a tame crow, but she was good.

"Now what you saying, Miz Tippen?" Sukey inquired with a return of manners.

But Mrs. Tippen was crafty.

"Ask me no questions, miss," she said tartly, "until you tell me what you got in your apron."

Sukey giggled. It was always a show how much the blind woman could guess. "How you know I'm toting in my apron?"

she asked.

"Apples?" said Mrs. Tippen, sniffing the air greedily and ignoring the question.

For answer Sukey lifted one of the red-skinned, frosty apples out of her apron and put it in Mrs. Tippen's hands.

"Sweet Lord," said Mrs. Tippen devoutly, turning her sightless eyes heavenward, "come out on the front gallery of heaven and bless that sainted Nancy Hart and her young'un, Sukey. She's done sent me apples — the very last she's got, without a doubt. That's sacrificial giving, Lord, and I want You to bless it. Amen."

The last word came out over a bite of apple and she turned to Sukey.

"Now I'll tell you what I was trying to say," she said happily. "I got company!"

"Company?" Sukey echoed the word. Nobody this far from the Broad River had many visitors. It was a thing the blind woman suffered from most. Since her boy, Tom, had joined the Army and gone to die she had been so alone — nobody to talk to, nobody to do

for. She wouldn't leave her cabin and go
and live in the Harts' crowded household
because she was stubborn and independent.
But she did yearn for company. Now somebody had come.

"Who you got for company, Miz Tippen?"
Sukey asked the question in an excited
whisper.

Still munching the apple, Mrs. Tippen
beckoned mysteriously and led the way into
her cabin.

"A lad . . . wounded in the swamp. I found
him when I went to the spring this morning. I
ho'ped him to the house — him a-leaning on
me, Sukey! — and I put him to bed. I made a
poultice for his leg, where the wound is, and I
fed him a little gruel. He's sleeping now but
when he wakes I'll give him an apple!"

Mrs. Tippen brought the last out with such
a rush of happiness Sukey felt a quiver of
shame that she had been reluctant to bring the
apples. She blinked her eyes to accustom
them to the darkness of the cabin and then the
fire on the hearth blazed up a bit and she saw!

On Mrs. Tippen's bed, his fine linen shirt plain to see over the best coverlet, his silver knee buckles gleaming below, there lay *a sleeping Tory*!

Chapter 2

If Sukey Hart hadn't been a daughter of the American Revolutionists' famed Nancy Hart she might have seen the sleeping Tory on blind Mrs. Tippen's bed without recognizing him. But Nancy Hart had carefully taught her eight children to spot the elegance, the British richness of the enemies of the American cause. They were, she cautioned them, to fear and hate the Tories like the sneaky copperheads that crawled in the woods.

Sukey was only ten years old but she knew that when you said "Tory" you automatically said "thieving-murdering-Tory." Now here was one sleeping away on their old neighbor's bed.

Sukey took a deep breath. She couldn't kill

him herself. She had never killed anything more'n mosquitoes from the river swamp. If she could just get her father, Benjamin Hart, or her mother. Ma could and would kill any Tory living!

Sukey turned swiftly to Mrs. Tippen.

"You stay here," she said softly. "I'll fetch help as fast as I can."

"Help?" the blind woman was puzzled. "Sukey . . ." Her voice rose and broke a little. "Sukey, he's breathing, ain't he? I thought I heard him breathing."

"He's breathing, all right," said Sukey grimly.

The blind woman let out a sigh of relief.

"Well, then set with me and wait," she said, happy once more. "When he wakes maybe he'll talk to us. A bit of apple might he'p him to feel like talking."

The lonely old blind woman said the word "talk" like a child about to get a play-pretty. She was hungry to hear talk, even Tory talk, Sukey thought bitterly. Well, she would wait, Sukey would, because she suddenly remembered that talk could be mighty important to the American cause. British soldier talk was so important, brave Nancy Hart had lashed a raft together and floated across the Savannah River, pretending to be a crazy woman, to hear and report it to the American side.

Maybe if Sukey could hear this Tory talk . . .

Mrs. Tippen was motioning her to a chair by the fireplace.

"Here, child, draw up," the blind woman directed. "We'll speak low so as not to disturb him and you can tell me how he looks. He's young, ain't he? And tall, like my Tom?"

Sukey gulped. Mrs. Tippen was trying to put this Tory in the place of her son the Tories had killed. She wanted to blurt out the truth but she dared not. The man on the bed might wake up and kill them both. Sukey winked hard to keep the tears from springing to her eyes. A daughter of Nancy Hart's wouldn't be a-crying. She mustn't let on to Mrs. Tippen that she had an enemy in the house until she thought what to do.

She turned toward the bed and obediently began to describe the sleeping soldier.

"Tall, I judge," she said, looking at the long hump he made under the hand-woven coverlet. "About Tom's size, I reckon."

"Fair, is he fair?" the blind woman urged her on.

Sukey looked at the blond head on the pillow.

"Fair," she admitted.

"His face, Sukey," Mrs. Tippen whispered, "is it bonny?"

Sukey studied the snub nose with freckles across the bridge, the fair eyelashes on the pale cheeks, the mouth. . . . She was dismayed to see the mouth suddenly quirking up in a smile. The Tory was awake!

Alarmed, Sukey backed closer to the hearth and the blind woman. The Tory devil might spring at them. Instead, he spoke.

"Not bonny, ma'am," he said to Mrs. Tippen. "But better than 'twas, thanks to your good treatment of me. I think I can be moving on now."

He shifted in bed and his face went white and a small sound of pain escaped his lips.

"No!" said Mrs. Tippen. "You stay put till you're well. Me and Sukey'll take care of you, won't we Sukey?"

Sukey hesitated and the boy's eyes were on her face — blue as her brother Benjy's, and pleading. Don't tell, he was saying mutely, don't tell.

Chapter 3

December wore on, cold and rainy, in Wilkes County, Georgia, that year of the American Revolution. There was fighting along the coast to the north and the great American general, John Dooly, had been killed in his bed as he slept.

Sukey Hart's mother, the daring Nancy Hart, was already well known to the Indians as the "War Woman" because of the way she fought the British-sympathizing Tories at every turn.

Even this creek was named for her, thought Sukey, balancing herself once more on the footlog across Wewatchee Creek. Wewatchee in Cherokee meant "war woman." If Sukey had told her about the Tory youth Miz Tippen had found wounded in the swamp and helped to her cabin, Ma would immediately have brought him to the American soldiers and maybe personally supervised his hanging.

But Sukey hadn't told Ma. She wasn't sure why. Old Miz Tippen's happiness in having the Tory for company in her lonely cabin was one reason. And there was another Sukey hardly dared admit to herself. The Tory was young, scarcely older than her brother Benjy, and wounded. His leg was improving slowly under the blind woman's poultices and herb baths, it was true, but not enough to enable him to run very fast or very far.

While he stays put, resolved Sukey, I'll not tell. But before he gets well enough to run, Ma'll have to know.

The blind woman was not out in front of

the cabin waiting for her that day and Sukey had a momentary feeling of fright. Could the Tory have killed old Miz Tippen and gone?

She ran the last few steps to the cabin and as she reached the door she heard the Tory's voice raised as one telling a tale. Sukey paused and listened.

"And they call it a Yule log," he was saying.

The blind woman, sharp-eared as usual, interrupted him. "Wait a minute, son," she said. "I think I hear Sukey Hart a-coming. You Sukey?" she called.

"Yes'm," Sukey answered meekly.

"Come right to the fire!" old Miz Tippen commanded. "I want you to hear this here boy talk. You know Christmas?"

Sukey murmured that she had heard of Christmas. It was the birthday of Jesus, that much she knew. But in those days in her part of the world there was no celebration of the day.

"Well, draw up," said Miz Tippen, "and hear. Start over, Edward," she ordered the boy on the bed.

"Edward Locke," the boy said to Sukey, smiling and inclining his head in a little bow.

"Sally Hart," said Sukey, giving her real name and making a small curtsy before she caught herself. (Curtsying to a Tory! What would Ma say?)

"I was telling Mrs. Tippen that this time of year makes me think of my old home," he said. "Getting ready for Christmas was the finest part of the year."

"Sukey, across the water they take on a sight over Christmas!" put in the blind woman eagerly. "They give presents to each other and deck up their cabins with green and have all manner of good things to eat. Tell her, son."

Sukey looked scornful. Bragging about his British home, was he, and the heathenish frolics they had? That took nerve, even from a Tory!

The stern churchmen in the back country, like the Puritans in New England, taught that it was sinful to celebrate on Christmas Day. In some parts of the new world it was even

15

against the law for a shopkeeper to close his doors and take a holiday. And as for feasting and exchanging presents . . . well, if it wasn't sinful, it was downright silly, Sukey thought.

"I was saying that where I used to live in England," the Tory went on, "today they would have ivy and laurel boughs and holly wreaths all over the house."

"Why?" asked Sukey coldly.

The boy on the bed smiled winningly.

"I'll try to tell you," he said cheerfully. "Everything about Christmas is done in remembrance of our Lord. Each little thing is supposed to be an act of worship and you must not have anger or hatred in your heart when you get ready for Christmas because that would offend Him. Every land has customs of its own — England, Germany, Sweden, Norway, Italy, Spain . . ." The boy's voice was dreamy.

"Think of it," murmured the blind woman by the fire. "All the furrin folks celebrating with gladness and us not even giving the blessed Jesus so much as a 'howdy' on

His birthday."

Sukey pulled up a chair by the fire and faced the Tory. "I'd like to hear about Christmas," she said meekly.

Chapter 4

Sukey Hart knew many things for a little girl just ten years old. She could spin and weave and help her mother cook for her father and six brothers and sister, Keziah. She knew how to speak enough Cherokee to talk with the Indians who occasionally came by her parents' cabin. And she could spot one of the wicked Tories, who fought for the king of England against the American colonists, a mile away, she thought.

She was confident of that. What she didn't know was how to keep her young heart from listening and expanding with warmth and happiness when she heard a wounded Tory youth tell about Christmas.

All one December afternoon in 1780 Sukey

Hart sat in blind old Mrs. Tippen's cabin across Wewatchee Creek and listened to Edward Locke, a Britisher born and admitting it, talk about how some folks away yonder across the sea celebrated Christmas.

"You know the story of how the little Baby Jesus was born in a stable in Bethlehem, don't you?" the wounded Tory began.

Sukey nodded. She didn't really know it very well. Her parents were good people but it wasn't until many years later that Nancy Hart would join a church. Ma told fine tales but not Bible ones.

"Tell it anyhow," urged old Mrs. Tippen, who dearly loved talk of any kind, particularly a story.

So Edward Locke told the story, which is now familiar to every child in Georgia and maybe most of the rest of the world. He told of the Baby's birth and how the angels sang and a great, bright star guided shepherds and wise men to the stable. He told of the gifts they brought the Baby Jesus, gold and frankincense and myrrh.

"In remembrance of that day," Edward went on, "people in many lands give presents to each other, especially to little children."

"Tell about St. Nicholas and the Christmas tree," ordered Mrs. Tippen.

So Edward told about the merry but mysterious old man who slipped around on the holy night leaving sweets and play-pretties for children — in their shoes in some countries, in stockings in others.

He told about how the people who didn't know about Jesus once decorated green trees to please the gods they worshipped. But when they learned about Jesus they placed stars on the tree in memory of the great bright one that had guided the wise men to Him, and candles because He was the Light of the World.

He told of the sweet cakes that were tied to the trees and the beautiful fruit, like the apples from Nancy Hart's fine orchard. He told of the food, the big goose that was roasted for dinner, and the great log that burned on the hearth all during the holidays, after a special blessing had been asked over it.

"Tell about the holly," directed Mrs. Tippen.

He smiled obediently. "Do you know the holly tree?" he asked Sukey.

Sukey nodded emphatically. The red-berried holly abounded in Wilkes County. She often gathered branches of it for her mother to make a special tea for sickness.

"It is sometimes called 'the holy tree,'" the Tory boy said. "Many people believe its leaves were used to make the crown of thorns when Jesus was crucified and it did not have red berries until some of Jesus' blood dropped on it.

"Since that day it has been used to decorate homes at Christmastime. In olden times people believed a sprig of holly over the door brought joy and peace to a house and protected the people within from bad weather like thunder and lightning."

Old Mrs. Tippen nodded. "I've heard tell of that," she said. "And witches, too, they used to say."

"I don't know about witches." The Tory youth smiled. "But they sometimes put a sprig of holly on the beehives to let the bees know it's Christmas. The old tale has it that the bees could not hum until the night of Jesus' birth, and then they learned. It's their way of singing.

"Wreaths of holly or any other evergreen are used at Christmas because they are round, representing God's mercy, and green, to stand for unending life."

Sukey's eyes were wide and bright.

"I want to celebrate Christmas!" she cried. "I don't believe it's heathenish at all. Miz Tippen, let's have us a Christmas!"

Chapter 5

Christmas of 1780 was but one day away as Sukey Hart sat before the big stone and clay fireplace and wondered how to go about making a celebration.

If I tell Ma about Christmas, she thought,

she'll want to know where I heard about it. And if I tell her from a Tory she'll march over there and haul him out of old Miz Tippen's cabin and get him hanged.

Even if he was a Tory — "thieving, murdering Tories" was the way Ma always called them — Sukey knew she did not want Edward Locke to be captured and killed. He was young and suffering from a wound in his leg. And besides — Sukey looked dreamily into the fire — he knew about Christmas.

On the way home from Mrs. Tippen's she had gathered red-berried holly to make a wreath for the cabin door and she was busy thinking of presents she could get together for her family. Her old corn shuck doll for her little sister, Keziah, and maybe Pa would help her cut cane from the creek and make whistles for Benjy and Lemuel and Mark. The older ones, Morgan and John and Thomas, were with the soldiers and if they could have some special Christmas food . . .

"Ma," she said aloud as tall, red-headed Nancy Hart stamped into the house with a bucket of water from the spring, "can we have us a Christmas?"

Ma looked at Sukey narrowly.

"What you talking about, child?" she demanded. "We got Christmas coming to us just like we got Saturday, Sunday, and Monday. Christmas comes and there ain't a thing we can do to halt it."

"I mean special," persisted Sukey, flushing awkwardly. "Like a frolic, kind of, with food and presents. It's the Lord's birthday," she ventured more hopefully, "and it don't seem right not to act glad about it."

Nancy Hart set the water bucket on the table.

"Well, young'un," she said thoughtfully, "I don't know. Old folks said it was heathenish, like worshipping idols, to celebrate Christmas. I never thought much about it, one way or t'other. But in these days when there's bad fighting and trouble and grief about, it would seem right good to have something to be glad about."

"Like Jesus getting borned?" Sukey suggested.

Mrs. Hart nodded and then her thin, homely weathered face became almost beautiful with one of her rare smiles.

"Shore, Sukey, we'll have us a Christmas. Pa and the boys will likely bring game home. I'll make a tater pone and sweeten it with molasses. You pick out hickory nuts and we'll see what we can do about a cake."

"Oh, Ma!" cried Sukey happily. "We'll fetch old Miz Tippen and could we" — daringly — "could we roast the gobbler?"

"The gobbler!" said Nancy Hart, astonished. "Sukey Sal, you've plumb gone out of your head! The gobbler's the only thing them thieving, murdering Tories have missed and he'll not be et up, Christmas or no Christmas!"

Sukey's face fell but only for a moment.

With Ma for it, they would have a Christmas anyhow. "I'll get the hickory nuts," she said and started for the door.

Before Sukey could reach the door there

was a pounding of horses' hooves on the road and then a shouting and a hurrahing in the yard. Nancy Hart reached the door first and threw it open as six Tories reined to a stop at the steps.

"We're looking for a British courier that passed this way three days ago," the leader said. "Where did he go? Have you seen him?"

"Would I be noticing Tory devils or telling them anything?" cried Nancy Hart. "I ain't seen none of your couriers and I better not. Git out of my yard!"

Sukey shivered with admiration and fear. They might hurt Ma, if they dared. The leader of the party looked as if he might dare. He was laughing down at Ma from his seat on the horse.

"This must be the famous War Woman, boys," he said. "Let's see how much fight she's got left in her. Woman, set us out some food!"

"I've got no food," said Nancy shortly. "Your kind has seen to that. Everything on the place killed and carted off and me and my little young'uns left to starve."

"Ho, not everything!" cried one of the Tories, spotting the gobbler in the yard. "We'll have us a turkey dinner."

He lifted his rifle to his shoulder and the cabin and Sukey were shaken with a mighty roar.

"Pick the turkey and get to cooking, War Woman," the Tory leader commanded.

And to Sukey's horror, her brave mother, the famous Nancy Hart, moved meekly to obey.

Chapter 6

The Harts' turkey gobbler roasted slowly on a spit over the fire and six Tories sat at the table drinking from a jug and making jokes.

Sukey Hart in all her ten years had never expected to see her mother so friendly with Tories. She didn't know which grieved her most — to have Tories come riding up and spoil what was to have been preparations for their first Christmas celebration or to see her mother acting meek and friendly with hated enemies. Now Nancy was leaning against the cabin wall, her arms linked behind her, laughing heartily at something the Tory leader had said.

Sukey sat by the hearth turning the spit and wishing she had never come home from blind old Miz Tippen's, where she had heard another Tory — a young and kind-seeming Tory boy — talk about Christmas. It had been so good, hearing Edward Locke tell about how other folks yonder across the sea had merry times on Christmas Day.

"You Sukey!"

Sukey was roused from her dreaming by her mother's voice, sharp and loud.

"Take the bucket and go fetch water for these gentlemen to drink," commanded Nancy Hart.

Sukey got to her feet obediently. Ma had changed some, she had, and Sukey didn't like it. To show she didn't like it she dragged her feet slow across the puncheon floor.

"Sukey, hurry!" cried Ma, grabbing her by

the shoulder. "Make haste, you hear me!" She pushed Sukey toward the door and then, glancing swiftly over her shoulder at the Tories, she whispered in Sukey's ear: "The conch shell, honey, blow the conch shell for Pa!"

The conch shell on the stump by the spring was always used to call Pa and the boys in from the fields but Sukey had never blown it before, particularly the special sobbing blast that meant trouble at home and usually brought them a-running. She didn't know if she could do it now but her feet carried her fast down the path to the spring, the bucket bumping against her legs.

Suppose she blew it and the Tories heard it? Suppose they knew Ma was not as friendly as she seemed and did something to hurt her? Sukey's heart beat hard in her thin chest and she was certain she would never make a sound come out of that old shell.

But Ma said to blow the conch shell and Ma knew what to do. Ma was still Georgia's great "War Woman," who helped her countrymen and was afraid of nothing! Pride gave Sukey strength and she took the old shell — grooved by its years of drifting against the sand on the ocean bottom — between her two hands.

Trembling a little she lifted it to her lips. She took a deep breath and let it go. The deep, sad note of the old sea shell rose and fell on the late December air — quavering a little at the end because, after all, Sukey was but a little girl and very near tears.

Twice Sukey blew into the shell. "A-whoo . . . a-whooee!" And then she put it back on the stump, filled the bucket at the spring and went running toward the cabin. There was a streak of light along the log-walled cabin and while Sukey went toward it, wondering, she saw what had happened. Ma had pushed the clay from between the logs and was slipping the Tories' guns, one at a time, through the crack!

Sukey had never held a gun in her hand before but she reached up and helped Ma get the next one through. Then she heard a commotion in the cabin.

"Look at the woman!" cried one of the Tories. There was a shuffling of feet and a scraping on the floor. "You treacherous old biddy, *drop that gun!*"

Chapter 7

Sukey Hart dropped the water bucket and darted for the cabin door. The Tories were going to kill her ma!

But Nancy Hart's voice rang out with anger and triumph.

"I'll drop a load of powder into your worthless hide if you come a step closer," she cried.

Sukey peered in the door to see Ma facing six Tories. She had relieved five of them of their rifles, while they sat at her kitchen table drinking from a jug and joking, and she held the sixth gun in her own hands, raised to her shoulder, ready to shoot. One moved toward her and Nancy Hart fired.

He dropped to the floor, wounded.

The others stepped back fearfully, looking helplessly at their wounded comrade.

"Anybody else?" invited Nancy Hart dryly. No one stirred but Sukey held her breath. There were so many of them and only one of Ma.

Suddenly she heard noise on the spring path and at the same time footsteps, limping but coming fast, on the path from old Miz Tippen's.

Pa had heard her conch shell blast — and so had the wounded Tory who had been old Miz Tippen's company!

A sob caught in Sukey's throat. He'll kill Ma or be killed, she thought. Either way it was more that Sukey could bear. She knew you had to hate a Tory but this one talked of Christmas . . . maybe if she ran to meet him and persuaded him to go back . . .

Sukey turned but it was too late. Edward Locke and her father, Benjamin Hart, reached the cabin at the same time and, to Sukey's amazement, rushed in together. Another explosion went off in the cabin and it was so thick with smoke Sukey couldn't tell what had happened for a minute.

Then she saw Pa and Edward Locke were holding guns and four of Ma's Tory prisoners were marching toward the door, dragging with them the two Ma had wounded.

"Don't shoot 'em, Ben, you and Ed," Ma was saying. "Shooting's too good for them. Save them and leave it up to our soldiers to decide what they deserve."

Ma put out an arm and hugged Sukey to her.

"You're a smart, peart young'un, Sukey Sal," she said proudly. "You blew the conch shell a fine blast."

"Was that Sukey doing that blowing?" asked Pa, smiling at her. "You couldn't have done it better yourself, Nancy."

Ma beamed at him and at Edward Locke. "Hurry with them thieving, murdering Tories," she said good-humoredly. "Sukey wanted to have a Christmas celebration and we just got time to get the other children and old Miz Tippen and plan us a frolic."

Sukey tugged at her Ma's sleeve.

"Ma, how did you know Miz Tippen's Tory?"

"Tory!" Nancy Hart's laughter exploded in the cabin and from the doorway Edward Locke and Pa joined in. "Why, Sukey Sal, Edward Locke ain't no Tory! British born, all right, but as loyal an American as you and me. He's the courier they come a-looking for."

Sukey let out a deep and happy sigh.

"Now fetch in the water and let's clean up," Ma said briskly. "Since the gobbler's cooked, we might as well eat him for Christmas."

On her way to get the water bucket Sukey found the holly she had gathered. She wasn't sure how to make a holly wreath but she meant to put some over the door anyhow, for joy and peace and safety from thunder and lightning and witches. Ma would protect them from Tories.

CHRISTMAS WEEK IN PRETTY VALLEY

Chapter I

THERE WAS NO
denying the December wind was cold. It
swept down into Pretty Valley, swooshing
and tugging at Henry Grady Huckaby's
frayed old coat and turning his nose and his
hands almost as blue as Stovelid Mountain,
which, anybody can tell you, is the bluest

of the Blue Ridge Mountains, winter or summer.

But Grady, riding the top rail of the lot fence as if it were Old Babe, the mule, noticed neither the cold nor the color. He was so excited he rocked and rolled on the fence like a cowboy in a western picture show.

Before him on the frozen ground in the lot, Jingle, the smartest teetotaling bull yearling in the North Georgia mountains, did tricks. Not ordinary bull yearling tricks, which consist mostly of eating and galloping stiff-leggedly about on a frosty morning, but regular Ringling Brothers, Barnum and Bailey tricks like you'd see in a circus.

"March, Jingle!" cried Grady and puckered up his lips and whistled "From the Halls of Montezuma to the Shores of Tripoli."

Jingle, standing straight and smart on his four legs, cocked a brown eye at Grady and obligingly marched about the lot fence, picking up his feet and putting them down, proud and military like.

"Dance, Jingle!" cried Grady and he wriggled about so he could pat his hands and beat time against the lot fence with his feet and began singing the old ballad:

> *"Diamond Joe come git me,*
> *The one I love's done quit me . . ."*

Jingle halted the march and went into the dance with a grace which warmed Grady like a hot brick next to his feet at night.

The cold air rushed into his mouth and hurt his throat but he sang on, watching with pride as Jingle dipped and do-say-doed about the lot, looking ridiculously like an overgrown mountain boy at a Saturday night frolic. For a second Grady thought of his brother, Robert Toombs Huckaby, called Toomy, who used to dance with the best of them at the Saturday night square dances, and he felt his throat tighten and heard his own voice falter.

He swallowed and righted his voice and then determinedly put Jingle into the best trick he knew. This was the trick to beat 'em all, the last one he'd taught Jingle and the one that was to be his present for Toomy on Christmas morning.

Toomy, who was sixteen and the oldest of the Huckaby children, had lain flat in the bed since summertime when he fell and hurt his back while he was putting new shingles on the barn roof.

Since Daddy had died, Toomy had been father to all of them — to Grady, who was nine and the next to the oldest, to Velma and Tamer, who were seven and five, and the baby, Tally (officially named Herman-Gene Talmadge Huckaby).

Toomy, their big brother, had been a tall strong boy who could plow Old Babe all day and laugh and sing and play the guitar from sundown until the moon rode high over Stovelid. Only he hadn't laughed or sung or even smiled anything but weak, pain-twisted smiles in so many months it hurt Grady to think about it.

"Toomy's back is hurt," Ma said, "but it's his spirit that's stubborn to heal. Thinking he might be a cripple and not be able to do for the rest of us is eating his strength away. If we could just hearten him up . . ."

"Christmas, Ma!" Tamer had cried. "Christmas is coming and Toomy purely loves Christmas! That'll hearten him."

But Ma had only smiled at the little girl, had shaken her head doubtfully and gone on hanging out the clothes. Grady, as next to the oldest, knew what the trouble was. Presents. There wouldn't be any presents in the Huckaby house this Christmas and without presents Christmas wouldn't cheer anybody.

He had thought about it for days. He and the little girls were well and could skip presents and the baby, Tally, was too young to care, but if they had a present that would hearten Toomy . . .

He owned nothing himself, did Grady. Neither cash nor goods nor even a changing of clothes. The only thing of value he owned in the world was Jingle, the bull yearling.

And whoever heard of giving a sick boy a bull yearling for Christmas? Yet a smart bull yearling like Jingle that knew his name and came when called like a good watchdog. *Maybe*.

That's when Grady decided to teach Jingle tricks, funny, marching, dancing tricks that would make Toomy laugh and cheer him up and somehow spur him to try to get well.

It had taken months. Grady had worked every morning and every afternoon after school, between chopping wood and gathering eggs and feeding Old Babe and the cow. And now one week before Christmas, Jingle was practicing his last trick.

Grady was so intent on the cream-colored little bull that he almost didn't hear Ma calling him. And then the wind blew from the house and he heard her voice, strong and clear, and he almost fell off the lot fence. When Ma right-named any of them it was important — and she right-named him now.

"Henry Grady Huckaby!" she yelled. "Make 'aste and get to the house!"

Grady tumbled off the fence, waved goodbye to Jingle and went a-running.

Chapter 2

Ma was standing on the back steps with her arms wrapped around her shoulders, hugging herself against the cold, when Grady ran up from the lot. Her plump pink face, always soft and ashine with love for her five children and all her neighbors in Pretty Valley, was drawn into tight little nets of wrinkles now. And although he was but nine years old Grady knew it was from worry.

"Yes'm, Ma?" he said, answering her last call politely.

Ma Huckaby, looking at her next-to-the-oldest boy in his frayed, too-small jacket and overalls with the wind tossing his sorghum-colored hair, let her face relax in a tender smile.

"You Henry Grady," she said softly. "You been pranking with your calf?"

"Oh, yes'm," Grady said in a rush of pride and pleasure, lowering his voice so it wouldn't carry to the shed room where Toomy lay sick under the cover. "You ought to see Jingle, Ma! He's the smartest teetotaling calf in the — "

"I know," finished Ma, "in the North Georgia mountains. But," she changed the subject and her face went sad again, "you going to have to leave him for a while, Grady. I want you to go into town and see Mr. Rakestraw for me."

"Mr. Rakestraw?" Grady repeated the name in awe. "Me, Ma?"

"You'll have to, Grady. I can't go and leave Toomy. He don't seem so good today. And the little girls kind of have to look after themselves and Tally. You're the next to the oldest and you'll have to talk business with Mr. Rakestraw for me."

Grady's heart sank. Mr. Rakestraw was the storekeeper in Tall Bear, Georgia, the man who had a mortgage on Old Babe, their mule. When Daddy died Ma had to borrow cash money from Mr. Rakestraw and the way Grady understood it, that gave him a hold on Old Babe until they paid up. Mr. Rakestraw was a tallow-faced man who didn't take up any time with children and he sucked on his teeth and made grunting noises when he talked to Ma.

"Go and see him," Ma went on, "and tell him Toomy's sick and we didn't make much of a crop without him to help. Tell him Ma said if he can let us have more time on Old Babe . . . till we can make our spring crop or sell some wood, we'll pay up sure and interest, too. You hear me, Grady?"

Grady nodded, swallowing hard. Without Old Babe . . . why without Old Babe, they couldn't farm at all! Old Babe pulled the plow. Old Babe drew the wagon and the syrup mill. She hauled the firewood down from the mountain. She broke the ground for the cabbage and corn and potatoes and took what they made into town so it could be sold. If they lost their mule, Old Babe . . . Grady couldn't bear to think of it.

"Make 'aste now and wash up," Ma said briskly. "I'll hitch Babe to the wagon and you take a load of wood and a basket of my canned vegetables and preserves to Mr. Rakestraw.

He won't take 'em for pay but it's Christmastime and it'll show him we're willing to send what we've got even if it ain't money."

Ma headed for the barn to hitch up Old Babe and Grady was dipping water into the washpan on the porch when he heard Toomy calling him.

The room was dim but Toomy's face was white against the red and gray of the turkey track quilt.

"Take my coat, Grady," Toomy said. "It'll be too big for you but it's warm and . . . looks like you're going to have to grow to it."

"Oh, no, Toomy," Grady protested. "You'll be well and needing your coat soon and I wouldn't want to dirty it for you."

A smile stirred briefly on Toomy's pale face but it was the kind of smile that flickered in his eyes and twisted his mouth without lighting them.

"Take it, son," Toomy said. "I may never need it again."

Hesitantly Grady took his big brother's jacket down from the hook on the wall and hung it over his own narrow shoulders. Did Toomy mean he would never get well? Did he mean that he, Grady, was to take on the job of big brother?

Resolutely Grady squared his shoulders. He wasn't afraid of Mr. Rakestraw. He would save Old Babe and then on Christmas Day when Toomy got Jingle . . . The thought made Grady feel so much better he drove out of the yard hunched down in Toomy's big coat and whistling cheerily.

Chapter 3

Mr. Rakestraw's store was the biggest one in Tall Bear and if he hadn't had to worry about the mortgage on the mule, Old Babe, Grady Huckaby wouldn't have liked anything better than to be in that store so close to Christmas.

In the middle of the store the distended sides of the heater were rosy red from the light'ard knots and hickory chunks somebody had been feeding it. And while Grady waited to see Mr. Rakestraw he stood and breathed deeply of the fine smells of the store. There were jars of peppermint candy and wooden buckets of fat chocolate creams and pink candy with cocoanut insides. Oranges and apples pushed against the slats of new wood crates. There were sacks of nuts; and when one of the clerks lifted the lid of a jar of mincemeat and began to dip it out with a wooden paddle, Grady's stomach turned over and his toes curled up in an agony of delight and longing.

Mr. Rakestraw was busy in the little cage that was his office to one side of the heater and for a while Grady was so taken up with looking at the store that he paid no attention to the talk.

Then he heard Mr. Rakestraw's voice raised in anger: "No ma'am! I can't give you any more credit, Christmas or no Christmas! It ain't my fault if your children are hungry. If I fed all the orphans and widows in North Georgia my own family would go hungry. I'm sorry you all are cold, too, but I ain't responsible for the weather."

Grady turned his head in time to see the Widow Willis come out of the little office. Her eyes were blurry with tears and her chin quivered but she walked out of the store with her head held high.

Grady knew the Willises and he knew how far Mrs. Willis would have to walk — all the way down Washwoman Creek to that little house perched on a rock ledge without a stick of firewood for the cutting anywhere around it! Grady knew she had three little children and knowing that they were hungry and cold pulled him away from Mr. Rakestraw's heater.

He ran after the Widow Willis and when he caught her she was walking more slowly with her head ducked against the wind and tears on her cheeks.

"Miz Willis! Miz Willis!" cried Grady. "Wait. Me and Old Babe will ride you home. Ma sent you some wood and" — his eyes sparkled with sudden inspiration — "some jars of stuff to eat!"

"Why, Grady," said Mrs. Willis, wiping

her eyes, "how did your Ma know?" Then she saw the wood and the basket of Ma's vegetables and preserves in the wagon and a smile came out and made prisms of her tears. "Thank the Lord!" she said. "Thank the Lord!"

All the way down Washwoman Creek, Grady talked cheerfully to Mrs. Willis to keep her from inquiring how Ma came to know her need and to send her such a timely Christmas present. He told her about Toomy's sickness and Jingle, the trick calf he was going to give Toomy for Christmas, and he even bragged a little about all the things Jingle could do.

It wasn't until he unloaded the Widow Willis and the wood and food at her back door and had driven off calling "Merry Christmas!" that he thought of Mr. Rakestraw again.

To have to ask that man not to take Old Babe away from them and especially now that he had given away the presents Ma sent him, made Grady's heart sink under his big brother's coat like a flint rock tossed into Washwoman Creek.

He could hardly bear to walk in the store and, as it happened, he didn't have to go very far. Mr. Rakestraw was waiting for him at the door.

"Ain't you Mrs. Huckaby's boy?" the storekeeper demanded.

"Yes sir," said Grady politely, pulling off his stocking cap.

"I saw you hanging around here," said Mr. Rakestraw. "Did your Ma send the mortgage money or have you come in to bring me the mule?"

"Neither, sir," began Grady. "We ain't got the money yet because Toomy — he's the oldest — fell off the barn and couldn't help with the crop. But if you'll let us keep Old Babe awhile we will get the money and pay you everything — interest, too, Ma said."

Grady's voice faltered but Mr. Rakestraw wasn't listening anyhow.

"Unhitch the mule," he said. "If you should get the money I'll let you have the mule back. I don't aim to be hard on widows and orphans but, by granny, I want what's a-coming to me. Unhitch the mule and tell your Ma she better send a bigger feller to fetch the wagon."

It was the final insult and as Grady unhitched Old Babe he had to hide his face against the rusty old mule's hide to keep the storekeeper from seeing him cry.

Chapter 4

As Grady walked home from Mr. Rakestraw's store in the cold December dusk, he tried to sort out in his mind the mistakes he had made. He had come into Tall Bear from the farm, wearing his older brother's coat and feeling like a big boy, prepared to get on the good side of the old storekeeper with presents of wood and Ma's vegetables and preserves and then to talk him into allowing them to keep their mortgaged mule, Old Babe, until spring.

Instead, he had gone off on his own and given the wood and the rations to the Widow Willis and here he was, without even the use of Old Babe to get home. Without the wagon, even. Mr. Rakestraw had even suggested that a bigger boy would have figured out a way to get the now useless wagon home.

Grady bowed his head to the wind and thrust his hands deep in the pockets of his brother Toomy's coat.

Far away, beyond Pretty Valley where he lived, Stovelid Mountain turned from blue to smoky gray as night settled on its wooded flanks. The wind toiled around it and Grady, listening, heard it moan.

When old Stovelid moaned, mountain folks said, it was going to rain. It meant the wind was from the east and was bringing in, across the soft peaks and humps of the Blue Ridge Mountains, Atlantic Ocean rain.

Rain, thought Grady miserably, was all he needed now. If it rained he would not have anywhere to work with the bull yearling, Jingle, and keep him practiced up on the tricks he was to perform for Toomy on Christmas Day.

But rain it would. He knew that because he could hear old Stovelid moaning just as plain.

Suddenly he lifted his head. Over the moaning of the mountain he heard another noise, loud and closer.

He glanced over his shoulder and scrambled from the road just in time to get out of the path of a man in a car. The car pulled up even with him and stopped and a white-haired, red-faced man in a checked suit leaned out the window.

"Hey, coat!" he yelled. "Hey, you big coat, where you going with that boy?"

Grady grinned shyly and said nothing.

"Your name Grady Huckaby?" inquired the man.

Grady swallowed and bobbed his head.

"Well, come shake hands with Dixie Arrowsmith!" boomed the man. "I'm a showman and I hear you got a show calf. That right?"

Grady gulped and finally found his voice.

"I've got Jingle, sir," he said. "He can do tricks."

"Maybe he's what I'm looking for," said the man in the car. "The Widow Willis told the teacher at Tall Bear school that you had a yearling that could take orders. I'm putting on a Christmas pageant for the folks in Gainesville. I put 'em on all the time, all around the country. But this one needs something it ain't got. I'm thinking about a live calf for the manger scene. You want to get in the car and let's talk business?"

Grady nodded dumbly and hurried to get in the car.

"Now if this yearling's any account at all," said the man, stepping on the accelerator, "I'll buy him off you. But let's go look at him."

"Buy Jingle?" stammered Grady. "Oh, mister, I wouldn't want to sell Jingle. I'm training him for a present to Toomy. That's my brother, Robert Toombs Huckaby, and he's so awful sick I think he wants to die. Jingle's for him to make him laugh and want to sing and pick the guitar again."

The words came tumbling out and Mr. Arrowsmith looked at Grady sharply.

"If this calf's worth money, boy, don't you think you ought to let your mother decide? Maybe she rather have the money."

Grady looked at the showman aghast. Money? Why of course Ma would want the money. Here he was going home without their mule or their wagon and not giving a thought to what they'd do, how they'd live without Old Babe. If Jingle was worth money . . .

Grady's mouth trembled and he sank back in Toomy's big coat, stricken and quiet. To give up Jingle, not to have a present on Christmas morning for Toomy! If he could have held back the car Grady would never have allowed it to arrive at his mother's door.

Chapter 5

All the Huckabys except the sick boy, Toomy, gathered at the lot fence with Mr.

Arrowsmith to watch the calf, Jingle, go through his tricks.

Ma had her old bonnet on her head and the baby, Talmadge, in her arms. The girls, Velma and Tamer, sat on the fence holding the lantern so it cast a wavering circle of light on the ground. Mr. Arrowsmith, the showman, turned up the collar of his checkedy coat and leaned against the gate.

"The way I see it," he said, "we could use a calf that could be still up on the stage for three or four minutes. That's when the Baby Jesus is shown in the manger for the first time. Then the shepherds and the wise men start arriving and I'd like for the calf to get up and walk over to the manger and, if possible, bow down like it was kneeling in worship. Think your yearling could do it?"

Could Jingle do it?

Why it was the trick, the very best trick Grady had taught him! Yet standing there in the chill darkness Grady wanted to shake his head. He wanted to say, "Why no, sir. That ain't anything Jingle could do."

He could say it because nobody knew he had taught Jingle such a trick. It was his and Jingle's secret.

But he looked at Ma's face there in the lantern light and he remembered how anxious and worried she had looked when he told her how Mr. Rakestraw took Old Babe. Then he had told her about Mr. Arrowsmith waiting out in the car and maybe wanting to buy Jingle and her face had lighted up and she had reached for her bonnet and said, "Oh, praise the Lord! One door never closes but what another one opens up."

Now Jingle was the door that was opening up for the Huckabys and Grady couldn't close it. Sick at heart, he patted the frisky, cream-colored little bull yearling on the flank.

"Sull, Jingle," he whispered. "Sull and stay sulled."

Obligingly Jingle folded his legs under him and lay down on the ground. He tucked his head to one side and closed his eyes.

Grady looked at Mr. Arrowsmith and Mr.

Arrowsmith looked at his watch. Grady didn't speak and Jingle lay very still. It was the trick he was to have done in the house for Toomy on Christmas morning.

The wind blew and the lantern swayed, raking the little group with its yellow light. And still Jingle didn't move.

Then Mr. Arrowsmith, still looking at his watch, nodded at Grady.

Softly Grady began whistling: "Joy to the world, the Lord is come!"

His whistling grew louder and more joyful, despite the heaviness of his heart. And Jingle got up and shook himself and pranced around in a little circle. And then before the old feed trough that Grady had been using to represent his brother Toomy's bed, Jingle stopped and bobbed his head once and very slowly folded his front feet under him.

He was kneeling before the manger.

The little girls, Velma and Tamer, let out a deep breath together. And Ma, her face shining, searched Mr. Arrowsmith's face eagerly.

"Ain't it the beatingest thing you ever saw?"

she asked softly. "Ain't it the beat?"

Mr. Arrowsmith took out a silk handkerchief and wiped his face. "Yes, ma'am," he said. "It sure is terrific!"

And then to Grady, "Son, you've trained yourself an acting calf. He'll *make* the Gainesville Christmas pageant!"

He turned to Ma. "Do you think fifty dollars is a fair price for him, ma'am?"

"Fair?" Ma caught her breath, her eyes on Grady.

"It's more than fair, sir," she said. "It's a gracious plenty to pay for a little old scrub woods yearling. It's more than we had to mortgage the mule for when my husband died. It would more than pay off the mortgage. But I ain't the one to say. My son made that calf worth your money. He done it out of love for his older brother. It's for him to say if the yearling's to be sold."

Grady stood there with his hand on Jingle's head where the little hard nubbins of horns were just beginning to be felt.

For him to decide? He looked at Ma in

astonishment. She would let him decide such a thing! She thought him grown up enough to tell what they should do. Slowly he took his hand off Jingle's head and faced Mr. Arrowsmith.

"We'll sell him, sir," he said chokily. "If you'll give Ma the money, I'll go get our mule in the morning."

Then, so they shouldn't see his face and he shouldn't see Jingle's, Grady broke and ran for the house.

Chapter 6

The rain that old Stovelid Mountain had moaned about the night before had begun to fall when Grady started home from Mr. Rakestraw's store, driving Old Babe and the wagon. He huddled down in his brother Toomy's coat and let the reins hang loosely in his hands. Given her head, Old Babe slogged rapidly through the falling rain, seeming happy to be headed for home.

Grady should have felt happy, too. He had paid off the mortgage Mr. Rakestraw held on Old Babe with the money the pageant man had given them for the calf, Jingle. And he had enough left over to buy some oranges and candy and a present around for everybody in the family.

Ma had told him to. They had a long talk by the fire the night before and Ma told him he did right to give the wood and the food to the Widow Willis instead of to Mr. Rakestraw who didn't need it anyhow. And she was proud of him for deciding to sell Jingle to save their mule.

"Things ain't always easy to decide, son," she said. "But when you begin to be able to decide them to the benefit of the most people, you are growing up."

"But Ma, what about Toomy?" Grady had asked sadly.

Ma sighed and shook her head.

"'Twould have been a fine present for him, the yearling would," she said. "I believe, like you, that seeing Jingle dance and march and bow down like that would have made Robert Toombs laugh and want to play his guitar again. But since we had to sell Jingle maybe it was best Toomy didn't see him or know how hard things were."

Grady reckoned Ma was right but deep down he had an aching sense of loss — for Jingle and somehow for Toomy too. He took out the harmonica he had bought for himself. Once he had dreamed of having one to accompany Toomy on the guitar when they made Jingle dance. Now he had one, newly bought with the money from Jingle, and it didn't seem so valuable.

But it was raining and cold and he thought to cheer himself up by playing. Back in the depths of Toomy's coat he licked his lips and held the mouth organ to them.

"Jingle bells, jingle bells . . ." the lively air was dragging and he stopped.

Behind him a horn was blowing, a bell was ringing.

Grady turned on the wagon seat to see Mr. Arrowsmith's car moving slowly toward him and, tied on behind with a bell around his neck, the yearling, Jingle!

Grady leaped to his feet in the wagon and pulled Old Babe off to the side of the road. He knotted the reins around the dashboard and was on the ground when the car drew up beside him.

"Hey, coat!" called Mr. Arrowsmith, leaning out the window. "Where you going with that boy?"

Grady grinned his relief. If Mr. Arrowsmith could make that joke again he wasn't mad or coming back for his money or anything.

"Grady, I want you to take care of this bull yearling for me," Mr. Arrowsmith was saying.

"Sir?" asked Grady, bewildered.

"I'll tell you why," said the red-faced man. "This blamed bull yearling won't perform without you. He ain't worth a continental to me without his trainer!"

"You mean you don't want him?" asked Grady.

"You're durned tooting I want him!" cried
Mr. Arrowsmith. "Gainesville wants him in
their pageant and if we hurry we can put him
on at Dahlonega and Elberton and maybe
Clayton too. I don't want to buy him. I want
to rent him and I'll hire you to be his trainer.
And next summer when school is out if
you've taught him other tricks, maybe we'll
take him on the road with a carnival. How
would you like that?"

To travel with a carnival? Grady's eyes
bugged out and his head whirled but slowly
he came back to earth.

"You mean you're giving Jingle back for
keeps and the money you paid is just for his
hire?" he asked.

"That's right," said Mr. Arrowsmith. "I
haven't got time to baby-sit with a frisky bull.
You own him. I've rented him for the Christmas pageant. After that we make a new deal.
All right?"

"All right," echoed Grady weakly. And
then he practically yelled. "Yes, sir, *all right!*
But after Christmas I'll have to ask my

brother, Toomy, about taking him traveling because then . . . then Jingle'll be Toomy's bull."

"Okay," said the man, laughing. "Untie him and take him home now. I'll see you tonight."

Grady untied Jingle and Mr. Arrowsmith turned around and drove off; but before they headed home to Pretty Valley, Grady picked a sprig of red-berried holly by the roadside and fastened it in the rope around Jingle's neck.

Old Babe, hitched to the front of the wagon, stepped high and happy. Jingle, hitched to the back of the wagon, pranced. And Henry Grady Huckaby, in his big brother's coat on the seat of the wagon, took out his harmonica and played "Joy to the World" all the way home.

THE GIRL WHO HATED CHRISTMAS

Chapter I

ARAMINTA MORLEY
stood at the office window of the Open Door
Mission and watched the December rain blow
in against her grandfather's sign.

"Open Door Mission," read the sign.
"Welcome All."

The mission sign was as plain and colorless

as the life of a preacher's family, Araminta decided, looking at it. Black letters on white with a dim light (because electricity was something to save) burning over the sign. The wind blew the rain straight at the sign and made it swing drunkenly and clank with an eerie sound.

As Araminta watched, the bright gold and red and green beer sign across the street winked on and off, staining the mission's dull sign with cheerful reflected light.

Araminta grinned with lively twelve-year-old malice and gave her blond ponytail a little toss. Grandpa disapproved of drink. So many of the people who came to the Open Door were drunkards. But even he had to admit the beer sign was the most cheerful thing on Dog Alley.

Dog Alley.

Araminta sighed. On city maps, and maybe a few street signs the residents had not knocked down and hauled off for purposes of their own, the street was called Dogwood

Drive. And maybe years ago when the houses were new and proud back of snowy wood lace galleries, maybe then there had been dogwood trees.

Now it was called Dog Alley and, as Slick, the night clerk liked to say, only the dogs were left — whipped dogs, stray dogs, and dead dogs.

Slick meant human dogs and Araminta sighed again. It would be so much easier if he meant real dogs. With a real dog you might accomplish something. Food and warmth and kindness could be given in moderation. And that was all that was needed. You still had something left over for yourself.

But Grandpa's "dogs"! The term was Slick's and Araminta felt guily even thinking of it. Grandpa, being a preacher, didn't get angry often but he would be very angry if he heard belittling talk about The Folks of the mission. You couldn't beat Grandpa, funny, stubborn old man. He believed in something called human dignity and worth. He really believed that everybody, even the dirtiest old drunk, the ex-convicts and the beggars, had a divine spark inside.

Araminta brushed at her ponytail again but it wasn't a lively, complacent gesture. It was slow and dispirited.

Sometimes she got so *tired* of Grandpa and his goodness!

Sometimes, especially at Christmas, she longed to be gala, giddily selfish. She wanted warmth and comfort around her. She wanted to see her sweet, tired mother looking smart and stylish again as she used to before Daddy died and they came home to Grandpa and the mission.

"It can't be wicked," Araminta whispered fiercely to herself, "to want something just for *us*. I don't want to have to worry about The Folks all the time. The late-comers don't even sober up in time for Christmas. And most of the others just droop around, eating and sleeping and saying it's the saddest season of the year."

"Lord . . ." Without intending to, Araminta found she was falling into Grandpa's habit of talking to Him. "Lord, look after The Folks, if You will. But give *us* something for a change. Let Grandpa and Mother and me have a happy Christmas."

Araminta may have added an "Amen." (Grandpa peppered his talks with his Friend with reverant "Amens.") But the hall door opened behind her, letting in a shaft of light.

It was Mother.

"'Minta, honey," she said, her soft voice high with surprise, "what are you doing here in the dark? Is anything wrong?"

Mother was not any taller than Araminta and, considering that she was terribly old, practically thirty-five, she looked pretty neat. She was slim in a gentle, curvy way that made even her skirts and sweaters from the old, prosperous days look good on her. Her hair was a deeper gold than Araminta's and although she wore it long in a smooth knot on her neck, capricious little tendrils slipped out and curled around her face.

If she hurried, before she got too old, Mother might marry again — somebody nice and rich and distinguished. But if she stuck around the mission the best she could do would probably be Tom, which was all right, really. Araminta had no objection to his mooning over Mother, except that, like Grandpa, he was a dreamy minister who planned to do mission work and thought being poor was fine.

Araminta grinned at her mother.

"I was just admiring the beer sign," she said impishly.

Her mother put a hand on her shoulder and shook it in playful rebuke. "You need a spanking," she said, "but come and help The Folks decorate the chapel."

Araminta made a face of cheerful distaste.

"Oh, joy," she said. "Are we going to do it in something stunning this year like chartreuse and pink?"

"You're going to do it," said Mother firmly, looking a little tired again, "in just exactly what the Auxiliary Ladies brought."

Chapter 2

Because she was twelve years old Araminta Morley was perhaps just the age to be cynical, even at Christmastime. Sometimes she suspected that the Open Door Auxiliary Ladies, the mission's main benefactors, used the mission and The Folks as a pious excuse for getting rid of unwanted junk in their closets.

She was positive that some of the clothes they sent hadn't been in use since the days of some silent old movie star named Theda Bara. And poor Miss Starry-Sky Higgins, although possible the age, was not the type for voluptuous Theda Bara fashions.

From her stepladder, where she struggled to loop a garland of green over the chapel door, Araminta thoughtfully regarded Miss Starry-Sky, who was picking over the strings of burned-out Christmas tree lights the auxiliary sent. She looked, Araminta decided, like an old bone one of the real dogs of Dog Alley might have buried, dug up, found unpalatable, and buried again.

A beaded crepe dress in a strange shade of violet hung to her crooked, skinny little frame — too skimpy and too ruffled. On the whole, Araminta decided, it looks like the paper frill on a lamb chop after the chop has been eaten And yet, because she reigned imperiously as queen of the Ladies Dorm at the Open Door Mission, Miss Starry-Sky had grabbed the dress when the auxiliary box came and nobody — especially nobody like Grandpa and Mother — had the heart to take it away from her. In spite of his being a minister and all wrapped up in running a mission for hungry and homeless people in a big city, in spite of having no raincoat or overcoat, Grandpa looked wonderful, Araminta decided. He was tall and thin and stooped now so his best blue suit, now threadbare, seemed too big for him. But there was something about him . . . Araminta's heart swelled with love.

"Hi, Grand," she called from the stepladder.

Grandpa smiled at her. Grandpa was

always pretty quiet in the chapel between services. He stood for a moment looking at the garlands of green and at the small Christmas tree in the corner with the lights which would not burn. There was a look of radiance on his face like he might be praying.

But it was quickly dimmed by The Folks.

"Oh, Mr. McIntosh," cried Miss Starry-Sky, hurrying over. "If any of these transient families in the private rooms get situated before Christmas, could I have a room to myself? When one has been accustomed to privacy it's so difficult . . ."

Grandpa put down his bundles on one of the folding chairs and started to answer her in his gentle, patient way but before he could deal with Miss Starry-Sky's need for privacy, the others were crowding around him.

Old Mr. Hunt had slipped on the wet pavement with his crutches while looking for work and one of them broke. He demonstrated by hobbling back and forth before the minister how pitifully immobilized he was with only one crutch. Fat Mrs. Dumas, who made a pig of herself at every meal and hid any extras that came into the mission under her bedclothes and in her shoes, whispered to him that one of the cooks, probably the new one because he was just out of jail, must be stealing the coffee and diluting the sugar. The coffee was weak and the sugar wasn't as sweet as it should be.

And Charlie Puckett, one of the younger men who had come stumbling into the mission faint and feverish one night with a worried policeman to help him, just stood at Grandpa's elbow, looking gaunt and hungry-eyed, waiting.

"Any word, Reverunt?" he asked at last.

Grandpa shook his head and held out a hand to detain Charlie while he listened to somebody else. But the young man suddenly said a rude and shocking word, shook off the minister's hand, and strode from the room.

Araminta, seeing a look of pain cross Grandpa's face, was outraged. She climbed down from the stepladder with her blue eyes blazing. Selfish, demanding, ungrateful things . . . every one of them!

It was for these people that they gave up their own Christmas. For them Grandpa did without a winter coat and Mother worked too hard and was hidden away from fun and nice people in a dreary mission. For them Araminta herself had lost the memory of what "merry" meant in Merry Christmas.

Suddenly she felt that she could stand them no more.

"I think you're all horrid," she cried, looking from one to the other. "And I hate Christmas!"

And bursting into tears, she ran from the chapel.

Chapter 3

Talk of spanking Araminta was not unusual around the Open Door Mission, where her grandfather, the Reverend Alex McIntosh was superintendent. But it was all in fun. After all, she was twelve years old and supposedly knew how to behave.

And yet the night that she cried out she hated Christmas she wished somebody would spank her.

It was not that she wanted to take anything back. She did think the people who lived at the mission were selfish and she hated Christmas. But up in the room she shared with her mother in the superintendent's quarters on the third floor she felt so lonely and miserable she would have welcomed even somebody wanting to punish her.

Nobody came.

At least Mother didn't come until she had cried herself to sleep. And when she awakened it was morning and Mother had already dressed and gone downstairs. She had missed the night service, too, and Grandpa would not like that. She heard them singing down there, all The Folks, as they did every night after Scriptures and Grandpa's talk. Only now it was the songs of Christmas and they made her very sad up in her room alone.

Slick, the night clerk, was just coming up the

stairs as Araminta went down to breakfast.

"Hi, baby," said Slick, but his tone lacked its usual buoyancy. "You okay?"

"So far," said Araminta dismally. "I bet I catch it this morning though. Oh, Slick, wasn't it awful of me to act that way? Are Mother and Grandpa very mad at me?"

Slick shrugged and yawned. "I wouldn't know, baby. Your mother looks blue enough to dye a shirt these days anyhow. I thought it was because she was busting up with Tom."

"Oh . . . Tom," said Araminta scornfully. "Mother's smart to skip Tom. Another preacher, like Grandpa. Another mission, probably like this one. I wouldn't let my mother waste herself on such a marriage."

"So I hear." Slick sniffed. "Well, you know everything, Miss Fixit. Tell your mother not to hurt — and your grandpa too. He's some-where now all cut up because Charlie Puckett tried to kill himself last night."

Araminta was shocked into silence.

She stood on the stairs looking at Slick, openmouthed. To throw away the gift of life

. . . that was a sin. Charlie Puckett wouldn't dare. Grandpa wouldn't have it!

She started to speak but Slick had yawned again and gone on. She went down the stairs, slowly, troubled.

Grandpa was not in his office and Mother was not at her desk outside his door. Araminta looked in forlornly and wandered on back to the dining room. The breakfast dishes had been cleared away but some of The Folks continued to sit — complaining about the weak coffee, Araminta supposed. She got a bowl of cereal and a glass of milk and returned to the table, feeling shy about sitting with them after her outburst of the night before.

But they paid her scant attention. They were so busy talking.

"And Mrs. Dumas was so upset she went into the pantry and ate every last one of them fruitcakes the Reverunt was saving for Christmas," Mr. Hunt was finishing an account. "So this morning they had to take her to the Grady — she's that sick."

Miss Starry-Sky Higgins, still in her

beaded violet crepe, was listening attentively and Araminta expected her to say something grand about the greedy ways of common people.

Instead she looked as if she were going to cry.

"I tell you, trouble's amoung us," she said softly. "That poor boy. All the time his heart hungering and us not knowing it. And now Mrs. Dumas, poor soul. People ought to help one another, Mr. Hunt. Mr. McIntosh and that dear, sad girl can't do everything for us all. Come with me to the chapel and let's talk to the others."

Miss Starry-Sky in her ridiculous hand-me-down finery led the way and Mr. Hunt, walking with difficulty with his one crutch, stumped along behind her.

Araminta watched them. What did they think they could do?

There was plainly nothing anyone could do. Christmas in a mission was bound to be perfectly dreadful. Everybody's troubles came home to roost. She didn't know what

Charlie Puckett's heart was "hungering" for. She didn't know why anybody should feel sorry for Mrs. Dumas for being a pig. And if her mother was a "poor, sad girl" it was no wonder — no money to spend, no home of her own, no nice presents.

A feeling of sadness and self-pity gathered in her throat and Araminta found she couldn't swallow any more cereal. What about me? Christmas should have been her time — and here she was, having no fun at all. The family didn't exchange many presents and with all the trouble infecting The Folks . . . If she just had some money she'd have some fun.

The solution to her problem came to Araminta so suddenly she put her spoon down with a bang that caused her milk glass to jump on the scrubbed tabletop.

The honor box.

Grandpa kept a few dollars in an old tin box on the office desk for anyone who needed it. The idea was to take what you needed and pay it back when you could.

Well, she needed the money. She needed some fun. What was to prevent her taking the money and going downtown?

Araminta didn't once think about paying the money back.

Chapter 4

Araminta never had taken any money from the Open Door Mission's box before, but she didn't really know why she shouldn't. All The Folks under Grandpa's care had access to it.

Grandpa felt that it was humiliating for them to have to ask for carfare when they went to look for work or to have to beg a stamp when they had a letter to mail, which wasn't often.

He always told them the money was there for all and they were to use it when they needed it and then replace if for others when they could. Grandpa was proud that box had never been really empty.

"And I won't empty it." Araminta promised herself righteously as she ran upstairs to get her coat. "I'll leave something . . . for seed. But I just hope it's got a wad of paper money in it today — lots of it."

Araminta stood before the mirror longer than she intended, trying to decide if she should change her hairdo from a ponytail and if she somehow could wear lipstick enough to make her feel made up without Grandpa noticing that she was. When she finally left the mirror and went downstairs she found the hall crowded with people.

Charlie Puckett was being helped up the stairs by Grandpa. And Mrs. Dumas, looking weak and pale, was sitting on the bench by the door facing half a dozen of The Folks.

Araminta watched Grandpa and Charlie enter the men's dormitory and then she heard Mrs. Dumas say, "I just want to tell you all I'm mortally ashamed." She wiped her eyes. "I knowed them cakes I et wasn't mine. But looked like when I woke up in the night and heard about that young feller being nigh to dying, I felt so bad I plumb had to eat."

She started crying in earnest now and some of The Folks tried to soothe her by patting her plump shoulder.

"And the worst of it," she moaned piteously, burying her face in her hands, "I never did like the taste of fruitcake!"

Araminta turned away in disgust.

Grandpa was coming out of the men's dormitory and Araminta followed him slowly into the office. Maybe he was mad at her. Instead of sitting down at his desk he stood at the window, his hands locked behind him, his back to her.

"Grand," Araminta said, "I'm sorry I was ugly last night."

"Yes, child," Grand said without turning, "I knew you would be."

"Grand," Araminta's hand played with the honor box and surprisingly she saw it held bills — three or four or maybe as many as eight. Her heart beat faster as she eased out the money with one hand and crammed it into her pocket. It felt fine there, crisp and fine.

"Look, Grand," she went on. "I am sorry for saying it but what I said is true. These people are hopeless. You can't do anything for them. Look how good you've been to Charlie Puckett and Mrs. Dumas and look how they turned out — a coward and a glutton."

The old man at the window was quiet and Araminta went on urgently. "Grand, why do you waste yourself on poor dependent people? If you had a nice church where respectable people went, wouldn't that be just as good?"

Grand turned and for a moment Araminta thought he was angry. His blue eyes blazed but his voice was gentle and patient. "The best example any of us will ever have, wasted Himself on poor people, child," he said.

"Oh, I know," Araminta hurried on. "Jesus. But, Grand, you're just human and you can't change them. They're always going to be a drag on you or somebody — shiftless, hopeless people."

Araminta's Grandpa's voice was stern. "Thou shalt not judge! Charlie is a troubled boy. He got in difficulties and lost his job and when he couldn't support his wife and baby he decided to run off and leave them. He loved them and he thought they'd do better without him.

"When he came here and got work I wrote to his wife for him and she hasn't answered — not yet. He's a sensitive boy and he is tortured by his guilt — more than I knew. What happened last night happened because I failed him. But thank the Lord," the minister's voice was fervent, "we've got another chance. He's going to live."

Araminta was silent and Grandpa went on. "Mrs. Dumas eats because she is frightened. All her family is gone. She has nobody of her own and she has been close to starvation. When the police brought her to us it was because she had fainted on the street from hunger. You've never had that happen to you, have you, Araminta?"

The question was asked gently. Araminta

shook her head mutely.

"You say I can't change The Folks." Grandpa's white eyebrows lifted humorously. "Of course, I can't. But with God's help they can change themselves. That was the first Christmas gift to all of us."

Araminta gulped.

"Well, g'bye, Grand," she said and turning, she walked toward the door. Looking back, her hand in her pocket, warm against the honor box money, she added, "Thanks for the Christmas Eve sermon."

Chapter 5

Mother was in the hall as Araminta started out the Open Door Mission to buy herself a holiday treat with the honor box money. She was helping Miss Starry-Sky Higgins and Crippled Mr. Hunt get into enough scarves and ill-fitting galoshes to make up for the fact that their thin coats were no protection against the damp cold.

"Oh, are you going out too, 'Minta?"
Mother asked, taking in her coat. "Well, walk
a way with Miss Starry-Sky and Mr. Hunt,
won't you? The streets are slick and they need
a strong arm to help them across Peachtree in
the crowd."

The prospect of walking down the street
with Mr. Hunt and his one crutch and Miss
Starry-Sky with a man's old battered hat on
her head and her violet dress flapping beneath
an even shorter moth-chewed old fur coat,
didn't invite Araminta. But she knew better
than to refuse.

They left together and Mother stood at the
door, smiling anxiously after them.

When they had gone a few yards Miss
Starry-Sky looked back furtively and
clutched Araminta's arm excitedly with one
of her clawlike hands.

"Don't tell anybody yet but we think we
know where Charlie Puckett's wife and baby
are," she whispered.

"You do?" Araminta asked without much
interest. "I thought he gave Grandpa their

address."

"Yes, but we think they've come to Atlanta," Mr. Hunt put in. "Last night when Old Looey was trying to sell shoestrings and razor blades to the late shoppers he got so cold he went in Terminal Station to get warm. There was a young girl with a baby in there. The baby was asleep but Old Looey said when he thought about it a little it seemed to him the baby kind of favored Charlie Puckett."

Araminta smiled uncertainly. "Well, that's . . . nice."

Miss Starry-Sky and Mr. Hunt looked at each other, their spirits dampened a little by her lack of enthusiasm. They resumed their halting. hobbling progress toward town.

Araminta walked beside them. Old dreamers, she thought. Not making any more sense than usual. If Charlie Puckett's wife were in the station she must be running away from him. Otherwise she would have answered Grandpa's letter or come straight to the mission. Besides, what made them think it was

Charlie Puckett's wife and baby? Just because
a bleary-eyed old peddler thought he saw a
resemblance between a sleeping baby and a
man who tried to commit suicide?

Araminta dutifully saw the grotesque-
looking pair across Peachtree Street and then
she left them with a polite goodbye.

In spite of the damp and the cold the streets
looked beautiful to her. Lights from the windows made a false sunshine in the gray
morning and the music pouring from the
loudspeakers sounded to her the way Christmas carols should sound. The majestic tones
of an organ swelling with the trained voices of
a big choir, instead of Mother's courageous
fight to get music out of the old chapel piano
and the quavering, tone-deaf voices of The
Folks.

Araminta walked down Peachtree Street
and looked in all the windows first and when
she had looked her fill that way she ventured
into the stores. She meant to have a milkshake
first but then she thought of Mrs. Dumas and
she couldn't.

Even when lunchtime came and went she didn't eat.

She felt sad somehow and not very hungry. She thought to cheer herself by buying a lipstick and some nail polish to match. But when the saleswoman came to wait on her she shook her head.

"I don't want anything," she said. "I'm just looking."

The honor box money in her pocket no longer felt crisp and good. She had not even counted it and now she didn't want to. She thought of Miss Starry-Sky and Mr. Hunt walking in the cold and the damp on their pitiful, fruitless little errand. They could have borrowed carfare from the honor box. But they didn't. They had left the money for the others, which was more than she did.

"They're better than I am," she thought with sudden wonder. "They may not accomplish anything for Charlie Puckett, but at least they're trying. They care."

Grandpa and Mother cared too, she realized with a strange, growing sense of humility. They didn't care about Christmas presents and a bright comfortable way of life. They cared about The Folks.

Araminta found herself out on the sidewalk, her feet hurrying toward the mission.

"Lord," she prayed silently, "Let me take back what I asked for. Give *them* something for Christmas, not *us*."

Chapter 6

Darkness had not fallen, but because of the chill gray mist the mission sign had been lighted by the time Araminta turned in Dog Alley. Somehow the plain little sign looked warm and welcoming to her as she hurried along.

Open Door Mission. Welcome All.

Araminta didn't even look for its cheerful neighbor, the bright beer sign, but hurried straight for the front door.

There was such a hubbub in the hall nobody noticed her arrival at first.

Charlie Puckett and a pretty brown-eyed girl sat on the bottom stairstep holding hands. Mrs. Dumas was back at her old place on the bench by the door, looking strangely peaceful and happy over . . . a baby!

Araminta looked twice at the baby, who was not asleep now but making delighted crowing noises in response to delighted gibberish from Mrs. Dumas. The baby *did* look like Charlie Puckett.

Miss Starry-Sky, who had forgotten to take off her man's hat but had added a corsage of Christmas ornaments to her beaded dress, fluttered all about, telling over and over again how it happened.

"When I heard Mr. Lewis tell about seeing a girl and a baby in the station, I said to Mr. Hunt here, 'We must act at once.'"

"I can't get over it, Reverunt," Charlie Puckett said, lifting his eyes to Grandpa. "Polly was looking for me all the time. That's why she didn't get your letter. And if these folks hadn't taken an interest and gone looking for her, we'd still be separated."

Grandpa smiled at Miss Starry-Sky and
Mr. Hunt.

"That's so," he said. "They tried, against
considerable chances of failure. That takes
faith, and courage."

Mr. Hunt ducked his head modestly. Old
Looey, wiping the dampness off his trays of
precious shoelaces and razor blades, smiled
with pleasure at his part of the affair. Araminta's mother, passing cookies and coffee,
was quiet but a kind of light — Grandpa's
kind of light — seemed to shine on her from
somewhere.

She brushed Araminta's forehead with a
kiss as she handed her cookies.

"Was it a good day for you, darling?" she
asked.

A good day? Araminta thought. No . . .
and then . . . *yes!*

"Yes, Mother," she said. "A lovely day. And
this is so good. Isn't it wonderful to have
them all so happy? Things are changing for
some of them, aren't they?"

Mother nodded. "Yes. Charlie and Polly

Puckett are getting jobs and Mrs. Dumas is going to live with them and keep house and look after the baby. She's so thrilled, 'Minta, to have a family to look after again."

"Mother . . ." Araminta was hesitant. "If you married Tom we would have a mission somewhere, wouldn't we?"

Mother looked away, her face not so radiant now.

"That's right," she said. "Tom's going into mission work."

"Well, look, Mother . . ." Araminta was shy. "I wish you'd marry him. He's nice and I *like* missions."

"'Minta" — Mother's voice was low and tender — "do you mean it? Would you be happy if Tom and I . . . oh, darling, I'd love to!"

When The Folks were all in the chapel, ready for the evening service, Araminta slipped into the office to return the wad of crumpled bills to the honor box.

It was dark in the office except for the light from the sign outside and at first Araminta

thought her eyes were playing tricks. She had
lifted the lid to the box and instead of coins
she had left for "seed" there was a fifty dollar
bill, the first Araminta ever saw.

"Grand!" she cried, running toward the
chapel. Then she stopped. He would be
beginning the service. But he wasn't. The
day's events had made him late. He was just
now coming down the stairs, his old blue suit
freshly brushed, his white hair shining, his
Bible in his hands.

"Look, Grand, what I found in the honor
box!" Araminta cried, holding out the
money. "Where did it come from?"

Grandpa looked at it, pleased but not
excited. Money to Grandpa wasn't so awfully
important.

"I think I know," he said casually. "Sometimes some of our folks go on from here to
what you might call . . . success." He smiled
whimsically. "A businessman who made a
new start here a year or so ago paid us a
call this afternoon. I didn't see him leave
the money but I expect he did. It happens

sometimes."

"Grand, does it?" asked Araminta, astonished.

"Oh, yes, I told you people can change," Grandpa said, smiling at her. "You never know who you are really helping when you do for 'the least of these.' Sometimes" — his tone was jaunty — "even capitalists turn up."

Grandpa hurried on to the chapel and Araminta followed. But The Folks began singing before she got there. It rang out, about as usual.

"O come, all ye faithful, joyful, and triumphant," with the piano needing tuning and Miss Starry-Sky's cracked soprano rushing pell-mell ahead of everybody else.

But somehow it had a beautiful Christmasy sound.

CHRISTMAS COMES TO SNOUT ISLAND

Chapter I

TUCK STANTON BAILED
the brackish water out of the bottom of his
skiff and watched the tired gray December
fog drift in from the ocean and wind itself
around the pilings of the wharf.

Bad on Gramp's rheumatism, he thought.
Make him cranky as the mischief. But Gramp

was cranky anyhow today, and for a reason even his seven-year-old grandson could understand:

Women.

Womenfolks, said Gramp, were a plague and a pestilence. He had moved to Snout Island twenty years ago to get shed of them. Now a passel of 'em had tracked him down and although he was seventy-six years old and peart as a fiddler crab, Gramp had started acting like a sulky child.

Tuck could hear him now rattling the stovelids and quarreling with the stove in the stern of their little one-room shack up on the high ground. Of course Gramp's quarreling with the stove was nothing new. Since his parents got blown away in a hurricane when he was a few months old Tuck had lived with Gramp and the first talk he ever remembered hearing was Gramp's quarreling with the cookstove.

To Gramp the cookstove was "She" — a mean, cantankerous female piece of house plunder that smoked and burned up his precious fatback one day and sulked like a possum and refused to fry fish the next day.

"Plague take you!" Gramp would yell at the stove and come stumping out of the house down through the marsh to the water's edge to cool off. And always in a minute the lapping of the river water, the salty-muddy smell of the wind and the call of the marsh birds would ease Gramp's anger and bring a look of peace and contentment back to his grizzled, toothless old face.

Gramp purely loved Snout Island, which may not be on your map of the Georgia coast but as far as Gramp is concerned is the main one of what some folks call "the golden isles of Georgia." It's a little hump of land shaped like a pig's snout with a ridge of dry land in the middle, running down to spongy marshlands on the side. On the ridge half a dozen old oak trees grow, as bent and twisted by sea winds as Gramp himself and maybe even older. Under one of these trees is Gramp's house, a snug, fine little place made mostly of boards picked up on the beach, patched with driftwood and palmetto fronds and two nice bright tin hotel signs that got blown overboard in a September storm one year and happily came to harbor on Gramp's roof.

On the port side of their house was Gramp's garden, which, in December, had nothing left but a row of long-legged-looking collard plants and last summer's bean poles. And beyond that was the chicken yard where one old rooster and half a dozen hens scratched dispiritedly in the morning fog.

Gramp had lived there since Grandma died and his independence began to be threatened by the widows and old maids at Palmetto Landing on the mainland. He fished and trapped for a living and guided some when he could find bass fishermen and duck hunters who were smart enough to leave their womenfolks at home. He may have been a little lonely at first but then Tuck came to live with him and Gramp was perfectly happy.

He took Tuck everywhere with him from the first. "Even when you was so little I had to tote you in my bait bucket," he used to tell Tuck. And Gramp took as good care of Tuck as he did his fishing equipment or his shotgun.

"Cleaned you and oiled you same as if you was a twenty-dollar reel," Gramp said proudly. "Didn't need no women to tell me nothing."

There had been no women on Snout Island, nor elsewhere in Gramp and Tuck's life. But now there were.

Two women had come to Snout Island — with trouble, Gramp said, riding the same tide!

The day before, some fishermen had come to get Gramp and Tuck to go out with them and Gramp had not noticed that there were women in the crowd.

"Dressed the same as men — pants and all!" Gramp said furiously when he discovered he had been deceived.

Tuck hadn't minded the women, when he found out they *were* women. One of them was young and had red stuff on her lips and smelled like flowers instead of fish.

She took on a sight when Tuck baited her hook and showed her where to catch speckled trout. Tuck was beginning to enjoy it until he heard the older one talking to Gramp.

"You mean the child doesn't go to school?" she was saying in a high, squeaky voice. "And just the two of you 'way out here on this island? Why, Mr. Stanton, that's not right! Suppose you became ill? You're an old man. Suppose you died? Don't you think you both — or at least, the child — should move to town where there are schools and churches and medical care?"

Tuck didn't hear what Gramp said but he saw what Gramp did. Gramp weighed anchor and made the fishermen go in.

He said the wind had changed and the fish wouldn't bite no more, although Tuck knew the wind hadn't changed and the fish were biting. Gramp told them goodbye and wouldn't take their money for guiding. The men looked puzzled and, over the sound of their motor as they pulled away from the island, Gramp and Tuck heard what they said, plain as day:

"Crazy old coot. Must be losing his grip. Maybe we ought to tell the juvenile authorities about the kid."

Chapter 2

Tuck finished bailing out his skiff just as Gramp called him to breakfast. If the fog lifted, the skiff would be all ready for him and Gramp to go fishing and that might cheer the old man out of the black mood he had been in since the two women happened, like a bad accident, to Snout Island the day before.

"Gramp, boat's ready," Tuck said cheerfully as he pulled out a chair and sat down at the oilcloth-covered table where Gramp had set out their usual morning meal of fatback, hoecake, and syrup.

"Needn't be," said Gramp glumly. "Ain't going nowhere."

"Aw, Gramp," protested Tuck. "The fog'll

lift. It's early yet."

"Ain't going to be no fishing today," Gramp said ominously. "We stay right here and you learn reading and writing and figgering."

"Reading and writing and —"

Words failed him and Tuck's mouth worked soundlessly like a mullet gasping for air. "Gramp!" he finished reproachfully.

"What do you think, you're going to grow up like a cannibal with no schooling?" Gramp demanded angrily.

"What do I need schooling for?" Tuck asked reasonably.

Gramp took a long time pouring more syrup out of the can in the middle of the table, catching the drip down the side of the label with his finger and daintily licking it.

"There's a lot of times when schooling comes in handy," he said carefully, at last. "You cain't even read the names on boats! How you gonna tell one boat from another?"

"Why, Gramp," said Tuck, hurt. "I know ever' boat between Cumberland Island and

Warsaw Sound! You know I do. Private ones and Coast Guard ones. Game and fish ones, barges and all. You know I do, Gramp!"

The old man took a different tack.

"Well, suppose you wanted to order something from the catalogue?"

Tuck knew the answer to that.

"You can read, Gramp. You'll do the ordering."

Gramp stood up, turned his back on Tuck and faced the stove, lifting the lid to poke in some wood and slamming it down furiously.

"I'm old!" he said at last and woodsmoke or something made his eyes water. "I'm even past my Bible allotment of threescore years and ten. I could die, Tuck, and then what? You want to be sitting around here in your ignorance and me dead?"

The old man was so mad Tuck tried to think of something to divert him.

"What's a Bible allotment?" he asked.

"Why the Bible says —" Gramp began and then he yelled. "*Bible!* When was the last time you read the Bible? Answer me that, boy. No, you don't need to! You ain't read nothing. You living here on this island in pure heathenish ignorance — and if them juvenile authorities come and separate us and take you off to the orfin's home and me off to wherever they bury old folks, it'll serve us both right!"

Gramp was slamming at the stove again and causing smoke to pour out into the room, but Tuck hardly even noticed it. The idea that he and Gramp could be separated, that they would ever leave Snout Island for more than a day's fishing, was so astounding he could not take it in. He could just sit there with his mouth open and his hoecake cooling on his plate, untouched.

Women, like Gramp said, sure were a plague and a pestilence.

Tuck sighed.

"Gramp," he said resignedly, "I'll learn schooling. You start me off and I'll try to get the hang of it. Can't be so much to it."

Gramp started to say something but he thought better of it, clamped his toothless old jaws together and began pushing the plates and cups to one side of the table. He and Tuck made a practice of letting the dishes sit till they needed to eat again but today the space on the table was needed for schooling.

"If I can find it," said Gramp rummaging in his old tin trunk at the foot of their bunk, "dogged if I ain't going to start you off in the Bible. That'll learn them durned women!"

Tuck looked outside and saw the fog was truly lifting. But inside, it seemed to him, the climate was gray and cheerless.

Fishing weather, and him fooling with a book!

Chapter 3

Old Man Stanton had taken care of his grandboy, Tuck, as he always said himself, "since he was not much bigger'n a cork on a cast net." He had taught him many things necessary to their life on Snout Island off the coast of Georgia and in every case he had been easy and patient with him.

A boy needs time, the old man was aware, to learn to caulk a boat, repair an oarlock, or hook a fish or scale one. You had to be easy when you taught a boy to handle a gun and patient when you taught him to wait out a high-circling formation of geese.

But the December day the old man undertook to teach Tuck to read and write, patience and gentleness forsook him.

"Tarnation!" the old man yelled. "Cain't you see nothing, boy? T-H-E . . . the! It's wrote there plain as the nose on your face, 'The book of the generation . . .'"

Tuck sighed. He'd been sitting around the oilcloth-covered table all morning, peering into the yellowed pages of a big old Bible book Gramp had hauled out of his trunk. Nothing about it made a grain of sense to him and if two women hadn't got mixed up in a fishing party Gramp was guiding and started pestering the old man about schooling, Tuck knew Gramp would never have thought of spending a pretty December day indoors.

As things now stood, Tuck was afraid if he

didn't learn to read he'd be hauled off to the
mainland to school — away from Gramp,
away from Snout Island, to nobody knew
what kind of dry-land existence. His head
ached from looking at the muddy confusion
of printing in the old book and a deep sadness
filled his seven-year-old heart.

Schooling made Gramp feel pretty desper-
ate himself. It had been many a long year since
he'd learned to read and he couldn't
remember how it was taught. To make up for
the unhandiness he was feeling, he hollered
and hit the table.

"Gramp," Tuck said at last, "it ain't no use.
Even if I could read them words they ain't a
bit of good to me. They don't make no sense.
I reckon . . ." His voice faltered and he felt
tears start up somewhere back of his eyeballs.
"I reckon you'd best let them orfin folks
have me."

Gramp stopped hollering and looked at
him. Then he gulped.

"It ain't so bad, son," he said at last.
"Readin's right interesting when you git into

it. We'll take it easy. Suppose I read you a chunk or two of this scripture and then maybe you'll get the hang of it?"

Tuck nodded, but without much hope.

Gramp cleared his throat and reared back in his chair and then for a while he floundered through some queer-named folks who "begat" some more queer-named folks. Tuck was too tired ask him what it meant.

And then Gramp hit a streak about a woman named Mary, a man named Joseph, and the birth of a baby named Jesus.

Tuck listened. He listened with more and more interest. Gramp paused for breath.

"Gramp, you reckon that's so?" Tuck put in. "That pore little baby . . ."

"What's so?" Gramp started to say. He looked at the Bible and looked at Tuck. His toothless mouth fell open and after a time he closed it and swallowed hard.

"Son," he said hoarsely, "I ain't got no more right to raise a boy like you than a jellyfish is got to a Jew's harp. I plumb forgot to teach you about Jesus!"

Tuck said nothing and Gramp pushed his cap on the back of his head and rubbed his forehead like it hurt him.

"Lord forgive me," he was muttering. "The time passed so fast and there was so much else you needed to know. Why, son, I've even let you miss Christmases . . . six of 'em . . . and here it is time for another one!"

Tuck smiled cautiously. This might be something else like schooling, something he'd just as soon miss.

"Christmas!" said Gramp, leaping to his feet. "Dogged if I ain't going to put you on a celebration this time! What day is this anyhow?"

Tuck didn't know. On Snout Island the names and numbers of days didn't matter. Sometimes Gramp looked at the almanac to check on seasons and tides. The old man grabbed the almanac now and studied it for a minute.

"December the twenty-fourth," he said softly. "Boy, we got to hurry!"

Chapter 4

"Be blessed if I recollect how we done Christmas."

Gramp Stanton stood in the door of his one-room shack on Snout Island and waved a broom uncertainly over the dust and rubbish on the floor.

"What's that thing got to do with Christmas?" his seven-year-old grandson, Tuck, asked, eyeing the broom suspiciously.

"Well, you clean up. That's one thing I remember," said Gramp forcefully. "When your daddy was a little boy your grandma made a big to-do over Christmas."

He looked uneasy. Gramp didn't like women and both he and Tuck hadn't lost sight of the fact that they had woman-caused troubles. But Gramp believed in giving the devil his due and he'd give women theirs.

"Womenfolks put a lot of stock in Christmas," he said. "And that's right. Cleaning up your house is a kind of way of putting your part of the world in order for the coming of the Savior. Now we're going to sweep and scrub and decorate the house. We're going to cook . . ."

Gramp looked at his ancient enemy, the cookstove, with distaste. "And I might even put a coat of blacking on Her," he added.

Tuck wouldn't have thought he and Gramp would ever be caught enjoying housecleaning. Cleaning a boat or a gun or even a fish was good work. But a house! And yet getting it ready for the first Christmas he ever knew was pleasant work because as they swept and scrubbed and raked the trash away from the door, Gramp talked of other Christmases and how folks celebrated.

He talked of the little Baby whose coming into the world that night was an event of such importance that it changed the lives of an old man and a little boy on a Georgia island hundreds of years later.

"I ain't told you about Jesus," Gramp admitted in a kind of shamefaced way. "I don't know how I come to overlook it except you was such a little mite of a thing when you first fell into my hands. And I got busy learning you other things. But I want you to know that I don't forget Him, and everything good and right I ever learnt you is owing to Him and His ways.

Tuck was spreading up the covers on the bunks and he paused to consider what Gramp had said.

"Did Jesus like a clean house?" he asked, surveying the straight room with the dishes washed and put on the shelf for the firsh time he could remember and the stove gleaming under its coat of black polish.

"We-ell," said Gramp, grinning. "He was a man and a fisherman at that. I reckon He woulda put up with a batch house, if you git right down to it. Clean hearts was what he said the most about — hearts clean of hatred and selfishness and filled with loving. Now, how's that?"

Gramp stood back to admire a bunch of bittersweet berries he put in a jar in the middle of the table.

Tuck moved beside him and they stood

together, admiring it shyly. It was the first attempt either of them had ever made to prettify the shack.

"Tell you what," said Gramp suddenly, "there's a bunch of little cedar trees over by Clabber Creek. We ought to have a Christmas tree even if we're without stuff to go on it this time. Cedar smells like Christmas. You take that bucket and a shovel and go dig up a little one, while I put that old hen on to roast."

"Chicken!" Tuck's face lit up. Gramp was a fish and fatback cook. Tuck could barely remember when they had had chicken before.

"I told you it was a prime celebration," said Gramp proudly. "Now make haste to git the tree before dark and I'll see what I can rustle up to go on it."

Tuck couldn't know that Gramp was worried about Christmas gifts because Tuck didn't know about Christmas gifts. All he knew, as he walked across the high ground back of the house toward the point where Clabber Creek cut through the marsh, was that he was happier than he had ever been in his life. The day that had started so drearily with worry and schooling had come to this: *Christmas*.

"Christmas . . ." He tried the word aloud and decided it was a mighty fine-sounding word.

And then he saw the boat, the little blue motorboat the women had come in the day before. It was back. The women who thought that he should be in some mainland school and that Gramp was crazy had come to get him!

Chapter 5

Tuck Stanton stood back of a clump of myrtle bushes and looked fearfully at the boat that had come sneaking in the back way, through Clabber Creek, instead of around by the river, to take him away from Gramp and Snout Island.

The shovel and the bucket he had brought to get the cedar tree lay on the ground, forgotten. Christmas, the day Gramp had joyfully brought forth, after having forgotten it for so many years, was nothing now.

The women had come to spoil it.

Tuck didn't know why the women would separate him from Gramp or how they had the right but he knew that Gramp feared them. Otherwise, Gramp wouldn't have started all that business about schooling this morning. Gramp hadn't thought that to be seventy-six years old was to be so old he might die. The women had thought of that and set a worry to aching in Gramp, a worry that only Christmas had eased.

Now they were back.

"Plague take you!" whispered Tuck fiercely, from his post back of the bush. "Plague take ever' last one of you!"

The boat, Tuck realized after a moment, was quiet. The motor was still. In fact, except for moving slightly with the current, the boat itself was still.

Tuck moved a little closer and peered curiously at the little craft. The women were on it, all right. But they were alone, no menfolks with them today. And what were they doing?

Cautiously Tuck slid down the bank toward the marsh. Then he saw.

The silly women had come in the back way and tangled the boat's propeller in the slick creek grass!

The older woman poked futilely at the marsh with a fishing pole, as if that might dislodge the boat. The younger woman, the one Tuck had liked, stood shivering on the deck, watching the fading light and wailing, "What will we do, Bess? It's getting dark! What will we do-o?"

I know what you can do, thought Tuck. You can stay here a little while till the tide starts running out and then you can drift out to sea. It would be a good thing, he thought, if they drifted out to sea and were never seen again. It would serve them right.

Tuck's foot slipped and he caught himself

on a clump of marsh grass, causing a movement which attracted the older woman's attention.

"Who's there?" she called. "There's something over there. Hello-o?"

She sounded so scaredy Tuck smiled to himself and then he felt sorry for her. He should set her mind at rest. He poked his head up over the waving golden grass.

"Oh, it's the child!" said the woman, relieved. "Little boy! Little boy! Is your grandfather with you? Run get him. We need help."

"Yes'm, I know it," said Tuck. And he saw the boat was beginning to turn now and to move slightly. The tide was running out He wouldn't have time to run get Gramp. The boat would be gone, swept out of the creek and toward the open sea before he could get to the cabin and back.

"Ain't you got airy anchor?" he called after the swaying craft.

"Oh, no!" cried the woman. "The anchor thing broke. It's why my husband wouldn't come. But we decided to come without him. Oh run, child, and get us help!"

"No time!" Tuck called to them. He could start. He could let them think he was going to get Gramp. They wouldn't know it was too late. And if they were swept out to sea in a little open boat with a snarled-up propeller and no power, they might never bother him and Gramp again.

Tuck started up the bank and then he turned. Gramp hadn't learnt him some things, maybe, but one thing he had learnt him for sure: when folks are in trouble, help them if you can.

The water looked cold. Dark was coming on fast and the mud in the creek was slick and tricky. But he had to try. It was what Gramp would have done.

Tuck kicked off his shoes and slid out of his jacket. He took his knife out of his pocket and opened the big blade. If he hurried before the current got any swifter . . .

He hit the water, feet first, in a leapfrog dive.

Chapter 6

Tuck came up for air three times and dived back under the disabled propeller each time. The water was icy and the knife felt clumsy and useless in his hand but he kept hacking away at the slimy ropes of grass that held the propeller and eventually he felt them give way.

The women were shivering and wailing like crippled sea gulls at the stern of the boat, but Tuck paid them no attention until he had finished with the grass.

Then he came up sputtering and allowed them to help haul him into the boat.

"Try the motor now," he directed.

The older one hastened to obey. The motor sputtered and then caught and they looked at him wonderingly.

"Oh, you marvelous child!" cried the one called Bess. "How did you know what to do?"

"It's what Gramp woulda done," said Tuck with dignity.

"Of course it is," said the younger woman warmly. "We were going to see your grandfather. We had some Christmas things for you. But I guess we got turned around in all these little inlets and canals and then the engine quit."

"Will you show us how to get there?" the older woman asked.

Tuck nodded, his teeth chattering in the cold. He might as well let them take him to the warmth of the cabin, now that they weren't going to drift out to sea anyhow.

"Turn here," he directed, "and swing wide. There's a mudbank."

Half an hour later Tuck huddled in a quilt by the shining black cookstove and watched the women put glittering ornaments and little packages on the cedar tree in the corner. Gramp had gone to look for him and brought back the bucket and shovel and the little Christmas tree. The room was warm and bright in the lamplight and the smell of cedar and roasting chicken perfumed the air. Gramp poured the women a cup of coffee and smiled and nodded as they told him what a smart, brave boy his grandson, Tuck, was.

"Well, I thank you," Gramp said at last. "Tuck learns right well, I think. He's tolerable clever."

"He certainly is!" cried the woman called Bess. "I don't mind telling you, Mr. Stanton, I underestimated your care of the boy. Why, I wouldn't have dreamed that a man and a boy living alone 'way out here on an island would have such a nice, attractive place. Just as clean as it can be, all fixed up for Christmas . . . why you even have the Bible right out handy on the table!"

"Gramp's teaching me to read out of the Bible," Tuck put in eagerly, while Gramp looked uncomfortable.

"Now Tuck . . ." began Gramp. "I'm not much of a teacher."

"That's another thing . . ." the woman said. "I had an idea of talking to you about letting Tuck come to Palmetto Landing and stay at my house and go to school. But I know you would never consent to that and, frankly,

I doubt if we could offer the boy anything to compare with what he learns from you. The way he freed our boat back there, why that was wonderful!"

"No," she went on in a moment, "Tuck ought to stay with you. But had you thought of sending him in to school with the Garrison boys? They live on Cowbell Island and they pass here every day in their speedboat. I know if we asked them they'd be glad to bring Tuck to school."

Tuck's heart sank. More schooling!

But Gramp's face shone like the little silver bells the women had put on the tree.

Tuck dozed a little while Gramp talked eagerly to the women of Tuck's future. And when he came to, Gramp was walking toward the door with the visitors.

Tuck heard him say an unheard-of thing. "Thank you for bringing him presents, ma'am. I hadn't figgered out anything like that. When you git right down to it, it takes a woman to make Christmas."

"You've done wonderfully, Mr. Stanton,"

the older woman said. And the younger one called, "Goodnight, Tuck, and Merry Christmas!"

"Merry?" Tuck tried the word in a whisper and then put it with the other one. "Merry . . . Christmas." They sure made a pretty sound.

THE LOST CHRISTMAS

Chapter I

SANDRA DUNSTAN LOOKED
around to make sure nobody was watching
her, then she carefully poured her milk into
the guppy tank. The milk mushroomed
slowly downward, leaving a widening cloudy
trail that blotted out the tiny fish, the
feathery water plants and the little stone

castle in the sand on the bottom of the tank.

Sandra, who was ten and should have known better, shook her soft blond hair out of her face and giggled softly.

She heard a noise behind her and spun around guiltily. Her older brother, Michael, who was twelve, had come into the breakfast room and was looking at the aquarium with interest.

"Save the women and children first!" he called out suddenly. He picked up a piece of toast and threw it into the tank.

"Oh, Mike, what fun!" cried Sandra. "Let's give them some oars. How about bacon?" She grabbed two pieces of bacon off a plate on the table and crisscrossed it on the toast.

"They need provisions, too," said Mike. "A shipwreck kit. Put in a little cereal."

Sandra threw him a delighted smile and picked up a bowl of oatmeal. "A spoonful for each guppy," she said, ladling it generously onto the soggy toast, which promptly sank from the weight.

"Too bad," sympathized Michael. "We'll have to launch another life raft. Here." He set another piece of toast afloat on the surface of the water.

"How about a grapefruit boat?" inquired Sandra. "Rub-a-dub-dub, three men in a tub!"

"Swell," cried Michael, throwing half a grapefruit into the tank with such vigor the cloudy, fish-smelling water splashed all over the floor.

"Quick, we need oil to pour on troubled waters," Sandra said and turned from the table to the sideboard where the cruet holding the vinegar and oil customarily sat.

At that moment Mrs. Hoyt, their father's housekeeper, walked into the breakfast room.

"Children!" she cried. "What are you doing to the poor fish? Quick, get them out of that slop!"

Michael looked from the plump gray-haired woman, whose always pink face was now red from annoyance and distress, to the puddles on the waxed floor. He smiled.

"Show us, Mrs. Hoyt," he invited. And then so softly only Sandra could hear it, he added, "Show us, as Hansel said to the old witch."

The words were no sooner out of his mouth than Mrs. Hoyt walked toward the guppy tank, her feet met the puddle on the floor, and she lurched and slid and sprawled flat on her back on the breakfast room floor.

Both children doubled up with laughter.

"Mrs. Hoyt, you're so funny!" cried Sandra. "You look positively cute!"

And Michael, who had anticipated the housekeeper's accident, was speechless with merriment.

That was the scene which met Mr. Daniel Dunstan's eyes on a December morning a few days before Christmas when he came down to breakfast in his home on Peachtree Road.

His housekeeper floundered awkwardly

on the floor, the guppies rose to the top of the tide of garbage in their aquarium and gasped their last. And his beloved son and daughter, who were, as he well knew, responsible for the whole mess, clutched their sides and laughed uproariously.

Dan Dunstan was a patient man, lonely since the death of his wife five years before, and normally soft-spoken. But that morning he let out a roar that caused his comfortable, handsome home to rock on its foundations.

"Shut up, you little monsters!" he yelled at his children as he hurried to help Mrs. Hoyt to her feet. "Shut up and get the mop!"

Now nobody had ever told Sandra or Michael Dunstan to get a mop before — and, odd as it may seem, that was really the beginning of the most remarkable Christmas they ever spent. That was the first step in the strange Christmas adventure of two of the most spoiled children who ever lived in Atlanta, Georgia, or elsewhere.

Chapter 2

If ever two children needed Christmas it was Sandra and Michael Dunstan. They needed it worse than Mrs. Hoyt thought they needed a spanking. They needed it worse than their exhausted and exasperated teachers thought they needed to be taken out of their elegant private school and committed to the state training schools for delinquents. Even their psychiatrist didn't really know how much Sandra and Michael had lived without really knowing about Christmas.

Only their father, tired and rich and sometimes awfully lonely, suspected the sad little secret about his children. Because their mother was dead he had tried to give them everything he could think of that children needed, including the most lavish Christmases money could buy.

Yet that December morning when they wasted their food and killed the guppies and stood by laughing while Mrs. Hoyt skidded and fell on the floor in the mess they made,

140

Mr. Dunstan realized that Sandra and Michael were ignorant, underprivileged little children.

"Did you realize that Mrs. Hoyt might have hurt herself?" he asked them after the housekeeper had limped out and they had sat down once more to a fresh breakfast.

Michael looked bland and innocent.

"Oh, no, sir," he lied.

"How about your fish," the father asked. "Did you intend to kill them?"

Sandra and Michael exchanged pained looks and Sandra rolled her eyes heavenward with a show of great boredom. Michael sighed heavily and pushed his untouched food away. They hated lectures and they planned not to listen if they could help it.

"I'm really surprised that you should behave so badly so close to Christmas," Mr. Dunstan went on.

Sandra laughed scornfully.

"You mean we won't get any presents?" she said. "Well, okay, don't give us any presents."

"There's nothing I want particularly anyhow," said Michael indifferently. "I've got a lot of junk you can have back if you want it."

Mr. Dunstan sat quietly a moment looking at his children — Sandra, a delicate little blond girl so like her beautiful mother, and Michael, strong and sturdy with bright close-cropped brown hair and fine blue eyes. They were handsome children and he loved them but they weren't any comfort or pleasure to him and he couldn't understand why.

He sighed heavily.

"I wasn't thinking of presents," he said. "There's something more to Christmas than that. I guess it's my fault you don't know. I tell you what . . ." His eyes brightened and he looked at them hopefully. "How would you all like to go away with me for a few days — just the three of us?"

"Where?" said Sandra. "California? I'd love to see the movie stars."

"Oh, California," sneered Michael. "Let's go some place decent for a change. I'd like a little excitement."

Mr. Dunstan looked at them sadly.

"I think we'll try the North Georgia mountains," he said. "One of the men at the office has a shack up there I think I can borrow. It's primitive. We'll have to do our own cooking and probably cut wood and haul water but it's very quiet and we'll have wonderful walks and talks."

"Oh, great," commented Sandra bitterly.

"*Some* Christmas," muttered Michael. "Of all the corny things to do!"

Chapter 3

Sandra didn't have any idea how long she had been riding when the headlights of the car picked up a little side road and her father slowed down and stopped. She was on the back seat with the boxes of groceries and covers and Michael was slumped down on the front seat, pretending to sleep because he had run out of sulky answers to his father's conversation.

"This must be the place," said Mr. Dunstan

cheerfully. "There's the big white pine tree with the lightning blaze on its face and there's the little creek. We've come about eight miles since we left the pavement — and that's where Sam said we'd turn off."

He maneuvered the car into the little side road and started moving slowly down a bank toward a creek.

"And there's the house," he said triumphantly. "This is the place."

"Where's the house?" asked Michael, peering into the woods.

"There," said Mr. Dunstan. "Two rooms and a screened porch. That's what Sam said."

"Call that a house?" said Sandra petulantly from the back seat. "Looks like a little shack to me."

"Dump," said Michael briefly.

Mr. Dunstan said nothing but concentrated on fording the creek and getting up the small hill beside the house. He parked the car and got out with his flashlight and keys to try the door. The door swung open and he turned to the car and called, "This is it, kids. Hop out and let's get unpacked."

"I don't feel so good," said Michael. "My side hurts again."

"Have we got to stay here?" inquired Sandra. "I'm so co-old and it looks so dark and scary. Can't we go back to a motel, Daddy?"

Mr. Dunstan opened the door and began pulling boxes and bundles out. "Let's give it a try, children," he said. "Come on. We'll build a fire and have the cabin warm in no time at all. I know you're hungry. Mrs. Hoyt packed us a nice lunch and there's a bottle of cocoa back here somewhere. Give me a hand."

Michael and Sandra climbed reluctantly out of the car and stood looking about them. The December moon was big and it threw a frosty light on the little cabin and the stiff winter grass. Somewhere behind them in the shadows they heard the icy tinkle of the creek. It sounded cold and lonesome and they hurried after their father into the cabin.

The beam of his flashlight showed a long, plain room with bunk beds in the corners and a big stone fireplace in the center. He found a kerosene lamp and lit it and then knelt by the hearth and began building a fire from the dry wood he found in the box by the chimney.

The flames leaped up and he hoisted a big gray log in place. Turning from the hearth he rubbed his hands together and faced his son and daughter, smiling.

"Poor babies," he said, reaching out a hand to draw each of them close to him. "You're tired and cold and sleepy. Sit here and warm up and I'll bring in the rest of our things and we'll eat something and go to bed. Tomorrow we're going to have a fine time. First thing in the morning I'm going to show you how to make the best flapjacks you ever put in your mouth."

"Ugh!" said Sandra, shrugging off her father's arm.

But Michael waited until their father had gone back out to the car again before he said anything. Then he said softly but determinedly, "Tomorrow, Sandy, we're going to run away."

Chapter 4

The morning was bright blue and silver — blue sky and frost-silvered earth with the bare branches of the trees making a delicate tracery of charcoal shadows against both earth and sky. But Sandra and Michael were too busy running away to notice that.

They left the little cabin before breafast, when the ring of an axe on the wooded slope back of the cabin told them their father was where he would not see them.

Now it was midmorning and the air in the North Georgia mountains was sharp and sparkling as a cut-glass goblet — and Sandra and Michael were hopelessly lost.

"My side hurts," said Michael, stumbling up a rocky slope.

"Oh, your side!" scoffed Sandra. "You're all the time using your side since you had your appendix out. Use it on Daddy and Mrs. Hoyt but don't tell me it hurts. I know better. You got us lost and a hurting side's not going to find us."

"Aw shut up," said Michael but without much heat.

He was hungry and worried. Somehow his sense of direction was off. It had been his plan to take a shortcut through the woods to the highway, where he knew he and his sister could hitchhike back to their home in Atlanta. That, he felt, would show their father that they did not intend to be pushed into spending Christmas in an isolated mountain cabin and listen to his lectures.

He smirked a little, thinking how even now Daddy would be searching for them and worrying, maybe even cursing himself, Michael thought hopefully, for bringing his children to such a place.

He stepped on a loose rock and his feet slipped out from under him, sending him sprawling among the rocks and briars.

Sandra began giggling, but a long thorny branch snapped back and hit her in the face, scratching her nose and drawing blood from her cheek. She cried instead.

Michael sat up and caressed his bruised

ankle with his hand. There was a time when he would have laughed at Sandra's tears but something — maybe his hurting leg or being hungry and lost — made him feel sorry for her.

"I tell you what, Sandy," he said gruffly. "Let's go back to the cabin where Daddy is. We probably got him worried enough. And we could get something to eat."

"Yes," said Sandra, gulping a little and wiping her eyes. "He was going to make flapjacks. But are you sure you know the way back?"

"Sure," said Michael getting to his feet. "We'll get back on that little creek and just follow it."

Sandra wiped her cheek where the salt of a tear caused the briar scratch to smart and smiled at her brother in real admiration.

"Let's go," she said.

They did go, slowly and painfully, with more briar scratches on their faces and arms and occasional falls where footing was tricky. They found a creek and began following it. A dun-colored cloud floated lazily off the top of a mountain and hung itself over the sun, turning the day from blue and silver to dull gray. They got their shoes wet in the marshy places along the creek and their feet grew stiff and ached with cold. Michael lost his cap and Sandra lost one of her bright red mittens.

The creek bank was a tangle of vines and dark green clumps of mountain laurel and rhododendron, so dim and jungle-like in places the children didn't realize for a time that it was growing dark.

When they came to a clearing and saw the light had gone from the sky, Sandra began to cry.

"Hush, Sandy," said Michael desperately. "Hush. I think I hear something."

And miraculously enough, when Sandra stopped crying he did hear something. He heard a whistled tune and the tune was the sweetest of all Christmas melodies — "Silent Night, Holy Night."

Just then as he and Sandra stared into the gathering darkness, they saw the tune came with a boy — a boy who was driving a cow along a path at the edge of the clearing.

Chapter 5

Sandra and Michael thought they had never seen a prettier sight in their lives than the house to which Pete Mills and his cow, Fancy, led them that cold December evening.

It was a humpbacked little house nudged up against a mountainside for warmth. It had no paint on its walls but a tendril of blue smoke from the chimney was busy skywriting a welcome over its roof. And its doorway, standing open, was a bright square of firelight.

They stood by the fireplace and felt the warmth of the flames steal achingly over their numb hands and feet while the voice of Pete's mother, who sat in a chair in the corner, warmed them with its welcome.

Her face was thin and pale but her voice was strong and hearty.

"Young'uns, git to stirring," she called out to the four little girls, all younger than Pete, who made a circle about Sandra and Michael and stood smiling shyly.

"We got company — Christmas company! You know how that banty rooster has been crowing all day. I told you company was coming and here it is! Ivy, set places at the table. Maybeth, warm up the leather britches and the crackling bread. Pete, hurry with the milking. Warm milk will taste good on a night like this!"

The children scattered as she spoke, throwing Michael and Sandra radiant smiles.

"Now!" said the mother. "Give the least ones your jackets to hang up and pull up chairs. We're the Millses. Them least ones is our twins, Katie and Laurie. They're little but the most he'p to me. Hand 'em your coats."

Shyly Sandra and Michael complied. Then Michael, because he was the oldest, gravely took upon himself the responsibility of an explanation.

"We're the Dunstans," he said. "I'm

Michael, she's Sandra. We live in Atlanta but
we were up at Mr. Sam Jackson's cabin with
our father and we . . . we got lost."

"Lost?" said Mrs. Mills. "Mercy! Is your
father lost too?"

"We don't know," faltered Sandra, suddenly thinking of her father, who might be
wandering through the dark woods, looking
for them "We left him at the cabin." She
looked anxiously at Michael. She didn't want
to tell this nice, welcoming woman they had
run away.

"Then you'uns is all right," said Mrs.
Mills, relieved. "He'll find you. I don't know
where that there cabin you're talking about is.
We seldom git over yon mountain. But
you'uns stay put and your folks'll find you."

She laughed. "Like I tell my chaps, a lost
bairn is a heap easier to find than a lost calf.
Bairns rare back in a clearing and stay still but
calves git the go-yonders."

Her tone was so merry Michael and Sandra
laughed in spite of their weariness and their
hunger.

"We'll make like a barn," offered Michael sturdily.

"Yes, do that," said Mrs. Mills. And then in a more serious tone she beckoned them closer to her chair. "I been sitting here praying the Lord would send the young'uns something fine and special for Christmas," she whispered. "I think you'uns come a-purpose to answer that prayer. I couldn't be prouder to see anybody."

Sandra and Michael looked at each other uncomfortably.

"We haven't got any presents," Sandra said apologetically.

"Presents!" cried Mrs. Mills, "Lord love you, we don't want presents. You brought yourselves. And hit's Christmas Eve. After you've et and rested we'll have ourselves a Christmas party!"

The leather britches — tender green beans which were snapped and threaded on strings and hung in the rafters to dry until they were pale gold — had been boiled with bacon rinds and a pod of red pepper and they tasted of sun and summertime. The crackling bread had been cooked in a pone so it was crisp outside but rich and moist with bits of lean pork inside. The milk, foaming and warm from the cow, Fancy, tasted so good Michael and Sandra could scarcely believe it was the same stuff they had poured in the guppy tank.

They ate and as they ate the young Millses stood watching them happily.

"When you'uns done eating," said Pete, "reckon you'll feel like coming out to the barn and he'p us with our surprise?"

Michael and Sandra answered the question in one breath.

"Sure!" they said.

Chapter 6

The twins, Katie and Laurie, stayed by the fireside with their mother, but Ivy and May-beth and Pete led the Dunstan children to the barn, shepherding them along in the light of the kerosene lantern.

"Hit's a Christmas tree we got," little dark-eyed Maybeth confided to Sandra in a whisper. "Have you'uns got a Christmas tree at your home?"

"Yes," said Sandra, thinking of the tall blue spruce which stood in the living room at home, decked with its strings of electric lights and glittering ornaments and scarcely noticed by Sandra and Mike in their boredom with Christmas.

"Oh, I know hit's a pretty one," said Maybeth politely. And Ivy, who was ten, smiled over her younger sister's head at Sandra.

"Wait till you see our'n," she said. "Maybeth's put the prettiest decorations of all on it."

Pete swung the barn door open and Michael and Sandra looked at the tree and swallowed miserably.

It was a little tree, straight and symmetrical, with its roots carefully packed in earth in a wooden bucket, but not a light did it have on it, not a glittering ornament, not a piece of tinsel, not a candy cane.

Paper chains cut out of the colored pages of the mail-order catalogue were draped over its branches. But the other things on it certainly were not colorful. In fact, they were almost indistinguishable in the lantern light.

"It's pretty," offered Sandra at last.

"Oh, hit ain't much to look at," said Pete offhandedly. "Hit's a smell and taste and feel tree. For Ma."

"For your mother?" said Michael, surprised.

"Ma's blind," said Pete quietly.

"Blind!" The Dunstans said the word together and then stared at Pete in horror and disbelief.

He smiled serenely. "Ma can see things a lot of folks can't see, but she can't see a Christmas tree. And she loves Christmas better than any time. We put the tree in a bucket so it would live and stay green and smell good and then we gathered up the presents she could smell and taste and feel. See?"

He drew Michael and Sandra closer to examine the little bunches of dried, sweet-smelling herbs Maybeth had tied to the branches, the bright chain of hot peppers from Ivy, and little bird's nest Pete himself had found last summer and saved.

There were packets of flower seeds from the twins and a bag of black walnuts they had picked up on the mountainside. Pete had put two arrowheads on a branch next to the base of the tree.

"Watch Ma when her fingers touch 'em," he exulted. "She'll know right off they're arryheads and she'll hold them in the palm of her hand and tell stories about the Cherokee Indians that used to live in these mountains and hunt with them things instead of bullets. Ma knows a heap of stories."

"What about the children?" asked Sandra anxiously. "Don't children get presents too?"

"Sure," said Pete sturdily. "Ma's got dolls hid away for the twins. Ivy and Maybeth had boughten dolls when our daddy was a-living and they give 'em to Ma to dress up all new for the least ones."

"Oh, I wish I could give your mother a

present!" Sandra said suddenly. And she didn't realize it was the first time in her life she had ever wanted to give anybody a present.

"Me, too," said Michael unexpectedly.

Pete and Ivy and Michael looked at them attentively. Finally Pete said to Michael, "Can you read?"

"Of course," said Michael, mystified.

"Good?" put in Ivy.

"Why, yes, I think so," said Michael.

The three Mills children exchanged delighted looks.

"Then you can read to Ma," said Pete. "We'll take the tree to the fire and have the party. And you can read Ma the Christmas story out of the Bible. She purely loves to hear it."

Michael grabbed hold of the bucket bearing the little tree and marched ahead, holding it triumphantly aloft. Sandra had to run to catch up with them but she grabbed Pete's sleeve at the steps.

"I . . . I could sing," she offered

breathlessly. "I could sing your mother a song."

Pete's eyes on her were bright with approval and gratitude.

"Why, that'll be a fine present," he said. "Fine as silk."

Chapter 7

All the rest of the Christmases they lived Sandra and Michael were to remember that Christmas Eve in a little house in the North Georgia hills.

When they had helped the Mills children haul their "smell-taste-feel" tree in to the fireside they placed it before the chair of the bright-faced blind woman who sat there. Then they all gathered at Mrs. Mills's feet on the floor for the presents.

Michael gave his present first — the Bible reading. Proudly little Maybeth brought him the worn family Bible and all their faces turned toward him, waiting expectantly. He had trouble finding the place in the Bible and his hands trembled and his voice quavered a little as he started, but as he read his voice gathered strength.

And the radiance on the face of the blind woman and the eager hush in the little room made the words seem to sing as he read them out:

"And, lo, the angel of the Lord came upon them, and the glory of the Lord shone round about them: and they were sore afraid. And the angel said unto them, 'Fear not: for, behold, I bring you good tidings of great joy, which shall be to all people.'"

"You see, children," said Mrs. Mills reverently, "that's the way it was. Oh, it was a wondrous thing the way we come to have Christmas! How could a body ever feel any way but happy knowing how He come into the world, the pore little mite of a thing!"

The children listened, and she talked over the details of the Baby's birth, making it seem as real to them as the firelight about them. It was to her a most loved story and she savored the words as she spoke them, pausing now and then to shake her head and smile at the wonder of it all.

Then she reached out her hands, the sensitive, seeking, work-worn hands of a poor blind woman, and Sandra watched them move over the plain little, grand little tree. They touched every gift upon it with so much love Sandra looked quickly at Michael to see if he noticed too.

Love, she thought, that's what Daddy was trying to tell us about Christmas. It's the loving and the giving that count. Not the presents, either poor ones or rich ones.

Pete brought a bottle of sweet apple cider out of the fruit house and Ivy fetched gingerbread from the kitchen. Sandra, who could tell from the solemn face on Michael that he was thinking of Daddy and wanted to see him too, put an arm around each of the twins and started singing. She sang all the Christmas carols she knew — the ones she had scorned in school and the ones she pretended not to know in church.

And then patiently she went back over the words and taught them to the Mills children.

The firelight hardly showed at all outside the house when the door was closed, so it must have been the sound of their voices lifted joyfully in the song "Angels, from the Realms of Glory" that guided Mr. Dunstan and his search party to the door.

And the welcome he got when Sandra and Michael heard his loud "Hello!" outside! They went tumbling out the door to meet him and drag him to the fire, hugging him and laughing and crying in a way the poor bewildered man hardly understood at all. If he had intended to punish them for running away he changed his mind. But that may have been because he saw something different in them.

When they rode down the mountain together in the back of the forest ranger's jeep, they leaned against their father and looked at the big bright star in the east. It seemed very close and bright and Sandra thought she knew what Mrs. Mills would say about it.

"That star," she murmured to her father, "has the most important story to tell."

Mr. Dunstan smiled and held them close. He knew all along the Christmas story is a love story.